WHY I QUIT
ZOMBIE SCHOOL

GOOSEBUMPS HorrorLand™

Also Available from Scholastic Audio Books

GOOSEBUMPS
HALL OF HORRORS

WHY I QUIT ZOMBIE SCHOOL

R.L. STINE

SCHOLASTIC INC.
New York Toronto London Auckland
Sydney Mexico City New Delhi Hong Kong

ISBN 978-0-545-28932-0

Goosebumps book series created by Parachute Press, Inc.
Copyright © 2011 by Scholastic Inc.

12 11 10 9 8 7 6 5 4 3 2 1   11 12 13 14 15 16/0

Printed in the U.S.A.   40
First printing, October 2011

WELCOME TO THE HALL OF HORRORS

THERE'S ALWAYS ROOM FOR ONE MORE SCREAM

Welcome. Step inside. You've found my old castle, even though it's hidden in the darkest, most distant corner of HorrorLand.

Yes, the Hall of Horrors is a special place. If you have a story to tell — a *terrifying* story — I am always here to welcome you. I am the Story-Keeper, the keeper of scary stories.

Come this way. Please — don't look so frightened. Those tarantulas don't bite.

They only nibble.

Take a chair in the fire. Oops. I mean *by* the fire.

Relax. Do you know why zombies like to sit down?

Because they're *dead on their feet*!

Ha-ha. Sorry. I shouldn't make jokes. I know you have a zombie story to tell me.

Well, this is the place for a good zombie story. I am the Listener. I am the Keeper.

"So you say your name is Matt Krinsky. How are you today, Matt?"

"Pretty good, I guess."

"What is that object you keep squeezing in your hand?"

"It's a rubber hand."

"A rubber hand. And you brought it here today because . . . ?"

"Because it saved my life."

"Well, I've got to *hand* it to you, Matt. You've got me interested already. Where does your story start?"

"In school."

"Please. Start at the beginning. Tell me your story."

"Are you sure you want to hear it? My school was the scariest school on earth."

Go ahead, Matt. Don't be afraid. There's Always Room for One More Scream in the Hall of Horrors.

2

I knew there was something wrong with my new school the first time I saw it.

My name is Matt Krinsky. I'm twelve years old. And I wasn't happy.

My parents say I have a bad attitude. They say I can take a bright, shiny red balloon and turn it into something tragic.

Well, balloons pop — don't they? That's kind of tragic.

Look, I admit it. I can see the horror in any situation. Or, as my dad likes to say, I always see the shadows on a sunny day.

He's always saying things like that. And let's face it, he doesn't mean it in a nice way.

My big sister, Jamie, teases me, too. She hates anything scary or dark. She can't understand why I love horror movies and comics and books. And she gives me a hard time because I collect every scary thing I can find. You know, masks and skulls and shrunken heads and movie posters. Cool stuff like that.

All four of us were in the car. We were on our way to my new school.

Bad enough we moved to a new town and I had to leave all my friends behind. Bad enough we moved into a tiny house *half* the size of our old house. Which means I have, like, *no space* to display my horror collection.

You know that scene in *Alice in Wonderland* when she grows really tall, so tall her head pushes up against the ceiling? That's how I felt in my new bedroom. No lie.

Could things get worse? Of course they could.

I had to go to boarding school for the first time in my life. Mom and Dad thought it would be a good experience for me. Can you believe that?

I wasn't happy. The whole thing was *scary* to me. What would the kids be like? What would the teachers be like? What would the *food* be like?

So many things to worry about.

The car rolled past empty pastures and fields. The crops had all been harvested. Nothing left but dirt and dead plants. Like gigantic graveyards.

"Just a few more miles," Dad said.

I sighed. "Why do I have to go to boarding school? There's probably a crazed maniac loose in the halls at night," I said. "Waiting in a corner with an axe."

4

"Matt, *you'll* be the only maniac there," Jamie said.

"Did you bring your axe?" Dad asked. Always ready to join in the Tease Matt for Fun contest.

"Give Matt a break," Mom said. "He's going to a boarding school for the first time, and he's nervous."

"I'm not nervous," I said. "I just know what goes on in these schools. There are *always* crazed maniacs in the halls at night."

"Too many horror movies," Jamie muttered. "They've rotted his brain."

"Romero Academy," I said. "What kind of a name is that?"

"It's supposed to be a good school," Mom said. "They have a soccer team. You'll like that, Matt."

"Only weird kids go to boarding school," I grumbled.

Jamie laughed. She poked me hard in the ribs. "*You* said it — we didn't."

"Don't touch me," I said, scooting away from her. "You spread disease."

Her mouth dropped open. "Disease? What disease?"

"The Jamie Disease," I said.

She dug her bony fingers into my ribs and started tickling me. She knows I hate it.

I twisted away from her. Easy for her to be happy. Her new school is two blocks from our house.

5

I pulled out a horror comic. I thought it would take my mind off Romero Academy. I studied the cover. It had a woman with green, decaying skin and deep gashes on her face. Blood ran from her empty eye sockets.

"Oh, yuck. That's *sick*," Jamie said. "Why are you reading that?"

"It's your life story," I said.

"There's your school up there," Dad called from the driver's seat. He pointed out the open window. "On the top of the hill. See it?"

I peered out the window. I started to answer — but I stopped.

Whoa. Wait.

Something was wrong. Something was terribly wrong. I saw it immediately.

The school stood at the top of a grassy hill. No trees nearby. It was a bright, sunny day. Sunshine made the grass sparkle all around.

But the school was dark, totally hidden in shadow.

How could that be?

"Wh-why is the school dark?" I stammered. I tapped Dad on the shoulder. "Look. *No way* can there be shade up there."

"It's bigger than I thought it would be," Mom said.

"It's very old," Dad said. "Built of stone. Looks like a castle."

6

"Don't you *see*?" I cried. "It's under a big shadow. But there's nothing to make the shadow!"

"Looks totally normal to me," Jamie said. She leaned over the front seat. "See what I'm saying? It's all the horror he watches and reads. It rotted his brain."

She chuckled. "Matt thinks he *lives* in a horror movie."

For *once*, Jamie was right.

2

An asphalt driveway curved around the hill. Dad
followed it up to the top. He pulled the car into a
small parking lot at the side of the building.

"Go take a walk and look around," he said.
"Mom and I will deal with your suitcases."

I climbed out of the backseat and stretched
my arms over my head. My legs felt stiff. It had
been at least a three-hour drive.

"Want me to walk with you?" Jamie called.

"Yeah. Like I'd want a second head," I said.

She made a face at me. "Matt, you're about as
funny as a runny nose."

"If your nose is running, you should chase
after it," I said.

It's a family joke. I thought it was a riot when
I was three.

I turned and walked along the asphalt drive
toward the school building. It was gray stone
with ivy growing down one shadowy wall. I

counted four stories, with a slanting black tile roof at the top.

Tiny windows poked out of the top floor. I wondered if that's where the students' rooms were.

A red-and-black pennant flapped in the breeze at the top of a tall flagpole. At least a dozen crows cawed and bobbed on the phone lines that fed into one wall of the school. Their cries grew louder as I walked closer.

It was a warm day for late fall. Many of the classroom windows were open, and I heard voices from inside.

From the far end of the building, I heard a band practicing a march. The band was *awful*. Squeaking and squawking. The crows sounded better than the band. I wanted to cover my ears.

The grass was high and patchy. Thorny weeds poked up everywhere.

Looking around the side of the school, I saw playing fields in back. Some kids were moving slowly across a baseball diamond. They weren't playing. Just walking.

I glimpsed a soccer field beyond the diamond. The nets were white and gleaming under the sunlight. No one back there.

A high black fence rose at the back of the soccer field. It had to be at least eight or ten feet tall. What was behind it?

Mom and Dad were carrying my suitcases toward the school. Jamie walked behind them, kicking a stone in front of her.

I saw a class sitting out on the grass. A dark-suited teacher paced back and forth in front of them, talking and waving a book in the air. I couldn't hear him because of the squawking band.

I stepped into the shade of the building. In a narrow courtyard, I saw a long line of trash cans along one stone wall.

It took a while for my eyes to adjust to the shade. When I could focus, I saw three boys. They leaned over a trash can near the back of the courtyard.

I stopped and stared. What were they doing back there? Why weren't they in class?

They didn't see me. They were huddled tightly around the trash can. One of them leaned over the side and pulled something out.

I strained to see what he had found.

He tore off a piece of it and handed it to one of the other boys. Then he tore off another piece and handed it to his other friend.

My mouth dropped open as I watched them start to eat.

No, it can't be, I told myself, squinting hard into the shadowy courtyard.

It can't be.

They CAN'T be eating a dead squirrel.

10

3

Mom, Dad, and Jamie came up behind me. I turned — and saw them staring at me.

"Matt — what's wrong?" Mom asked.

I pointed into the courtyard. "Those boys —" I choked out. "They — they're eating a dead squirrel!"

Everyone turned to the courtyard.

I gasped. No one there.

I squinted into the shadows. The three boys had vanished.

Jamie laughed. "Good one, Matt."

"No. Really —" I started.

"No more horror stories," Dad said. "Save it for Creative Writing class."

He had two suitcases under one arm and a carton of my stuff under another. Groaning, he lumbered toward the school entrance.

Mom shook her head. "We know you have a good imagination," she said. "But why make up crazy stories now? It's really not a good time — is it?"

11

Jamie laughed again and gave me a hard shove into the stone wall. She hurried to catch up to Mom and Dad.

I gazed into the narrow courtyard. My eyes went down the long line of trash cans. Dark in there. Too dark to see clearly.

Suddenly, I wasn't so sure I had seen three boys eating a dead squirrel. My eyes had to be playing tricks on me. My eyes and my brain.

A few minutes later, I stepped through the tall, dark wood doors of the school entrance. The front hall formed a circle. A tall statue of a black bird stood in the center of the circle.

It took me a few seconds to recognize the bird. A vulture. Its head was low under hunched shoulders. It was crouching as if ready to attack. Its dark eyes stared straight ahead. Its beak was open.

A red-and-black banner on the wall read: GO, VULTURES.

I saw Mom, Dad, and Jamie carrying my stuff down one hall. I started after them. But a tall, bald man in a loose-fitting gray suit stepped into my path.

His head was the color of an onion and kind of shaped like one, too. His eyebrows, his lips — his whole face was all the same pale shade, except for his eyes, which were yellow-green.

He flashed me a wide smile. "Are you Matt

Krinsky? I'm the principal, Mr. Craven. Welcome to Romero."

"Thanks," I said.

"I hear you're a soccer player," he said. His strange eyes locked on mine.

"Yeah. I played at my old school," I said.

"The Vultures can use you," he said, nodding his round head up and down. "You'll have to try out."

"Okay," I said. "Sounds good."

In the hall behind him, a group of kids moved slowly. Lockers slammed. Voices echoed down the long, curved hallway.

Mr. Craven turned and called to a dark-haired girl in a purple sweater and short black skirt. "Franny?" He motioned her over.

Franny closed her locker and came walking toward us, her eyes on me.

"Do you have a few minutes?" Craven asked her. "This is our new victim. Oops. I mean *student*." He laughed, a weird dry laugh. His yellow-green eyes flashed. I guessed that was one of his favorite jokes.

Franny smiled but didn't laugh. Maybe she'd heard it before. She had a nice smile. She tossed back her dark hair with a shake of her head.

"Hi," she said to me. "I'm Franny Roth."

"Can you give Matt a quick tour?" Craven asked her. "His parents are unpacking his stuff in his room."

13

He turned back to me. "This school is very big and confusing, Matt. Everything goes in circles. Don't want you getting lost in some endless hallway and disappearing forever. Ha-ha."

Another joke?

"I can give him the tour," Franny said. She smiled at me again. "Hope I don't get us *both* lost!"

A teacher called to Mr. Craven. The principal turned and strode away. He was tall and walked stiff-legged, as if he was on stilts.

Strange dude.

Franny led the way down the hall. I saw classroom doors and long lines of metal lockers on both walls. Kids moved slowly. I guessed they weren't in a hurry to get to their next class.

Franny waved to some girls in red-and-black cheerleader outfits. Just past them, a tall, skinny boy kept groaning and slamming his locker door with both fists. I guessed it was stuck or something.

"Have you gone here a long time?" I asked.

Franny nodded. "Yeah. Pretty long."

"What's it like?" I asked.

"Dead," she replied.

I waited for her to say more, but she didn't. So I said, "What do you mean?"

"You'll get used to it," she answered.

Huh? What does THAT mean?

Three boys edged past us, eyes straight ahead. They seemed to be stepping in slow motion.

14

One of them did a funny frog croak, and the other two laughed, then copied him. All three of them croaked like frogs as they moved down the hall.

The air was cold and damp. The whole hall had that gym locker-room smell. You know. Sweaty and musty.

"Why is everyone walking so slowly?" I asked Franny.

She kept her eyes straight ahead. "Silly question," she muttered.

"No. Really," I said. "Why is everyone walking in slow motion?"

She frowned at me. "Don't make stupid jokes," she said.

We turned a corner. I wanted to ask Franny to explain.

But two huge dudes stepped up and blocked the hall. They had to be twins. They were tall and very wide. They had short blond hair and enormous heads with huge ears that looked like they would flap in the wind.

Their black T-shirts stretched tight over their massive chests. Standing side by side, they filled the whole hallway.

"Are you the new kid?" one of them boomed.

I started to reply — but a choked cry escaped my throat.

I stared at their eyes. They had no pupils. Their eyes were solid white.

I lowered my eyes. I didn't want to stare. They probably got a lot of stares, I decided.

"Uh . . . yeah. I'm new," I finally said.

"He's Matt," Franny told them. "Matt, this is Wayne and Angelo. They're twins."

"Duh. Like he couldn't figure that out!" Wayne said.

"Our parents could never tell us apart," Angelo said. "We used to change names and fool them. A lot of times, if one of us got into trouble, the other one got punished."

"We thought it was a riot," his brother said. They bumped fists. Their knuckles were nearly as big as my hand!

"Once, Wayne pretended to be me for an entire week," Angelo said. "We were in different classes. He went to mine and I went to his. The teachers never knew."

I hardly heard what he was saying. I tried not

to stare, but I couldn't look away from those blank white eyes.

"So you play soccer?" Angelo asked. He leaned over me. He was like a *mountain*.

"Yeah. At my old school," I said. "I —"

I didn't finish because a girl called to the twins. They swung away and lumbered over to her.

As soon as they were gone, I turned to Franny. "What's up with their eyes?" I whispered. "They're totally white."

Franny squinted at me. "So?" she replied.

5

I was beginning to feel a little confused. Franny's answers to my questions didn't exactly make sense. But now she was staring at me as if *I* was the one who was being weird.

Wayne and Angelo strode back to us. Wayne waved Franny away. "We'll take over the tour," he said.

Franny nodded and gave me a thumbs-up. "Catch you later," she said. "Good luck." She disappeared around the corner.

Wayne put a big hand on my shoulder. It felt like he was pushing down on me with a baseball glove. "Show you the gym," he boomed.

We rolled through the hall. Kids actually slunk out of the way. Wayne and Angelo pushed through everyone like tanks.

We climbed a tall set of concrete stairs. The Dining Hall stood at the top. I saw a lot of kids in there having an early lunch.

"It's open all day," Wayne said. "You have your breakfast there. And lunch. And dinner. Unless you go out."

"Go out?" I asked. "You mean you're allowed out?"

"No, it's not allowed," Wayne replied. "But you can go out."

They both stared at me with their blank eyes.

Was Wayne making a joke? I didn't know whether to laugh or not.

Angelo scratched one side of his face. His skin was nearly as pale as his white-blond hair. "You like to prowl?" he asked.

I thought hard. "Prowl?"

"Yeah." Both guys nodded.

"Uh . . . sometimes," I said. My head was spinning. I didn't know what they were talking about.

"Well . . ." A grin spread over Wayne's face. "Then you have to go out, right?"

"Right," I muttered.

I suddenly heard a terrible groan from the Dining Hall. Choking sounds. Someone heaving and groaning.

Was some kid in trouble?

Wayne and Angelo didn't seem bothered by it. They didn't even turn to the door.

"The gym is up here," Angelo said. He gave me a gentle push. "It's a good gym. Everything is pretty new. And Coach Meadows still has the juice."

Did I hear right?

"Still has the *what*?" I asked.

Wayne pushed in the gym door with a big fist, and I followed them in.

I heard shouts and the thump of a ball on the hardwood floor. In the middle of the gym, younger kids were playing a volleyball game.

I stepped beside Wayne and Angelo and watched them play. The boy who was serving swung his hand up slowly and popped the ball over the net. The players on the other team lurched awkwardly toward the ball. Hands slapped wildly at it. Too late. The ball hit the floor.

Wow, I thought. *Everyone is so slow. If they all move in slow motion like that, I'm going to be a SUPERSTAR here!*

"Coach Meadows isn't here," Wayne said. "He only teaches the older kids."

"He'll be at our practice after classes," Angelo said. "We'll put in a good word for you."

"Thanks," I said.

I glanced back at the volleyball game. These kids were really lame. They needed to get moving, to get their energy up. It looked like they were all sleepwalking.

"We have soccer practice in the afternoon and usually at night after dinner," Wayne said. He leaned over me. "You don't have night problems, do you?"

I swallowed. "Night problems?"

He shrugged his big shoulders. "Sometimes I get moon fever," he said, lowering his voice to a whisper.

Moon fever?

"Like when the moon goes dark," he said, still whispering. "Not when there's a full moon. A full moon, I'm there. I'm really there. Know what I'm saying?"

I nodded. "For sure."

Angelo snickered. "My brother is totally weird."

Wayne shook his head. "Angelo gets the fever, too. He just won't admit it."

The volleyball came bouncing across the floor toward us. I picked it up and tossed it back to the players. "I have to go find my family," I said. "Is there more to the tour?"

Wayne pointed to a red door. "That's the locker room," he said. Then he motioned to the green door farther ahead. "And down that hall is the Reviver Room."

Again, I wasn't sure I heard right. "Reviver Room?" I stared at the narrow green door.

He nodded. "You know. In case you need it."

I've always heard that twins are strange. That they live in their own world. Wayne and Angelo were definitely proving it.

21

I've read some good horror stories about twins. One twin is always good, and one is evil.

But Wayne and Angelo both seemed like nice guys. I guessed that being identical like that just made them strange. All that talk about moon fever and a Reviver Room had to be some kind of private joke that the two of them only shared.

"We'll take you back to your family," Wayne said. We headed back to the gym doors. The volleyball game continued in slow motion behind us.

We made our way down the hall, which was crowded with kids coming from lunch. A few of them called out to the twins.

As we came to the stairway, I saw a book on the floor that someone must have dropped. I guess Wayne didn't see it. Because he stepped on it — and it slid out from under him.

Wayne let out a cry, and his arms shot straight up into the air. He toppled into the stairway, struggling to catch his balance.

And fell hard, headfirst.

His head made a *craaack* as it hit the concrete step. On the next step, I heard a sick *splaaat*.

Wayne groaned. Then he plunged down the whole stairway, his head thudding on every step.

I opened my mouth to scream, but no sound came out.

A strange silence fell all around me.

I peered down the stairs. Wayne lay crumpled at the bottom. Like a wadded-up ball of paper. He didn't move.

Angelo stood beside me, gazing down at his twin. He didn't speak. He didn't move.

I expected him to fly down the stairs to help Wayne. But he just stood there staring blankly. He didn't look upset. He didn't even look surprised.

My heart thudded in my chest. *Come on, Wayne — get up! Come on, move! Move your arms, your legs!* I couldn't speak. I couldn't move.

A group of kids gathered at the bottom of the stairs. Everyone stared down at Wayne in silence. No one screamed or cried out or dropped beside him.

No one did *anything*.

And suddenly, almost without realizing it, I began screaming: "HELP him! Somebody — get help! HELP him!"

Angelo squinted at me. Like he was trying to figure out why I was screaming.

His face was still totally calm. And he made no move to hurry down to his brother.

Finally, I saw two teachers appear downstairs. They pushed through the silent crowd of kids. They unfolded a canvas stretcher and placed it on the floor next to Wayne.

"Is he okay? Is he ALIVE?" I screamed.

For some reason, a few kids laughed.

What was funny about it?

The teachers didn't examine Wayne or anything. They rolled him onto the stretcher. His body was limp. His arms dangled over the sides.

The teachers strained to lift the stretcher. Wayne is a big dude. Finally, they raised him off the floor and carried him away.

My heart was still pounding. And I heard the sick *splaaat* Wayne's head made against the concrete steps again and again. I couldn't force that horrible sound from my mind.

I jumped when Angelo put a big hand on my shoulder. He finally spoke: "Hey, Matt, it's a good thing you came to Romero. We'll need you to replace Wayne on the soccer team."

Huh?

My mouth dropped open.

"Angelo," I said in a shaky voice, "Wayne is your brother. Aren't you worried about him?"

Angelo shrugged. "You know how it is."

I caught up with my parents and Jamie in my room. The room was just big enough for a narrow bed, a dresser, and a tiny desk.

"The bathroom is down the hall," Mom said. "Can you handle it?"

Do I have a choice?

Jamie sat on the bed, texting someone on her phone. Dad gazed out the tiny square window, down to the playing fields below. Mom was stuffing my T-shirts into a dresser drawer.

"Listen to me!" I cried breathlessly from the doorway. "Something is totally weird!"

Jamie looked up from her phone. "Your face?"

"Don't make jokes," I said. "Something *horrible* just happened."

That got their attention.

I told them about Wayne. "His head hit the steps hard, and he fell all the way down. He just lay there at the bottom, all crunched up. He didn't move."

"How awful —" Dad started.

I raised a hand. "No. Wait. I'm not finished."

I told them about how Angelo didn't move. "His own twin brother," I said. "He didn't shout or scream or call for help or anything. He just stood there. Like it was no big deal. None of the kids acted upset. None of them."

"Matt, you must be exaggerating," Mom said.

"No, I'm not!" I insisted. My head felt like it was bursting. I wanted to pace back and forth. But there was no room.

"I'm telling the truth," I said. "No one even bent down to see if Wayne was okay. It seemed to take *hours* for the teachers to arrive. And they just loaded him onto a stretcher and carried him away."

"It said on the website that they have nurses on duty here twenty-four hours a day," Dad said.

"That's not the point!" I screamed. "The kid didn't move. His head was cracked. I heard it. And no one checked him out. And all the kids . . . they . . . they weren't even upset."

Jamie gazed up from her phone again. "They were in shock," she said. "I studied it in Psych class."

"Huh?" I stared at her. "Jamie, listen to me. His own twin brother didn't even flinch. He —"

"He was in shock, Matt," Jamie said. "The kids were in shock. That's what happens sometimes when people see something shocking, something

27

totally horrible. It's like their brain freezes. It doesn't compute."

"Jamie is probably right," Dad said. "They won't react till later. Then it will hit them. The brain is funny. Sometimes it protects itself from —"

"I don't believe it," I said, shaking my head. "No way. If you were there, you would agree with me. It wasn't normal. It was totally weird."

Jamie snickered. "There you go again, Matt. You're in this school for ten minutes, and what do you do? You have to turn it into a horror movie."

Dad turned his gaze out the window. "Hey, look. A soccer game," he said. "Are you going to try out for the team?"

He was changing the subject. I could see I wasn't getting anywhere with them. I decided to shut up.

After lots of hugs and promises to call every day, they left. I watched them walk down the long hall, then disappear down the stairwell.

Silence. I dropped onto my narrow bed, my brain whirring.

My first time living away from home. My first day in a new school with all new kids and teachers.

Did I feel lonely? Not exactly. Instantly homesick? Not really. Afraid? No, not at all.

I couldn't describe how I felt. I just knew I was kind of emotional. I didn't feel like crying. But I knew I'd start crying if I let myself go.

I decided that setting up my room might cheer me up.

I'd brought a carton of my horror collection stuff. I knew I wouldn't have much room. So I just brought my favorite things.

I had one bookshelf above the desk where I could put things. I pulled out my scale models of my favorite classic horror movie monsters. I had Frankenstein and Dracula, of course. Perfect replicas of the original movie characters. And I had a nice-looking Godzilla and a Wolfman with real animal fur on his face and back.

My cousin works at the SyFy Channel. He sent me posters of their crazy monster movie characters. He sent awesome posters of Sharktopus, and Mansquito, and Frankenfish. I had just enough wall space to hang all three.

Fixing up the room made me feel a little more at home. But I still felt kind of weird.

I took out my monster-makeup kit and stood in front of the mirror over my dresser. I always liked to scare Jamie by making up my face, turning myself into a hideous ghoul or monster.

I started to dab black makeup around my eyes. Then I made my face pale white. I marked in deep ruts in my skin to make it look like my flesh was coming apart.

I don't know why I started turning myself into a ghoul. I knew Jamie wasn't around to scare. It was just something to do, I guess. Something to remind me of home.

Or maybe I could stagger down the hall and scare a few kids. It might be a way to meet some new friends.

I colored my lips black. And I painted a stream of bright red blood trickling down my chin.

Not bad. I looked like a creature who had just come back from the dead.

I was admiring myself in the mirror when I saw someone reflected in the glass. In the mirror, I saw her appear in the doorway to my room.

Franny. The girl I'd met when I first arrived at school.

She was staring at my back. She couldn't see my face.

I'll give her a little scare, I decided.

I spun around quickly, my eyes wide, my mouth hanging open.

And waited for her scream of surprise.

"How's it going?" Franny said. She took a step into the room.

I froze, openmouthed, my eyes deep in black sockets, bright blood trickling down my ripped-up face.

Franny glanced around the room. "Awesome posters," she said. "Did you see the one about the half boy, half spider?"

"Uh . . . sure," I said.

Jamie would have screamed her head off. What was up with Franny? She acted like my face was totally normal.

Why didn't she ask me about it?

"Are you learning your way around this place?" she asked.

I shook my head. "Not really." The makeup was starting to itch.

She picked up my Wolfman statue. "Want to take a walk? I could show you all the classrooms and places you need to know."

"Yeah. Great," I said.

Why is she being so nice to me? Did the principal tell her to help the new kid out?

"Let me just wash this off," I said, pointing to my face.

She squinted at me. "You mean it's *makeup*?"

"Ha-ha. Very funny," I said. I grabbed a towel and headed down the hall to the bathroom.

A few minutes later, we climbed the stairs down from the dorm rooms and began to make our way through the twisting halls.

"I guess Wayne and Angelo didn't give you a very good tour," Franny said.

"It was okay," I said. "But then Wayne took that terrible fall."

I shuddered. Once again, I pictured him rolling down the stairs, his head hitting every step. Once again, I heard that horrible *splaaat* sound.

"Did you hear anything about how he's doing?" I asked.

Franny bit her bottom lip. "Not good," she said softly. "They took him to the Reviver Room. But it didn't take."

I stared at her. "Excuse me? It didn't *take*?"

"Yeah. You know," she replied.

"No. Not really," I said. "I'm the new kid, remember? Tell me what goes on in the Reviver Room."

She studied me for a moment. I couldn't tell what she was thinking. Did she think I was out of it because I didn't know what a Reviver Room is?

"You go in that room if you are getting low or if you are damaged," she said finally. "And the Reviver turns on the power."

We turned a corner. Franny waved to a group of girls. Two of them were up on ladders. They were hanging a red-and-black GO VULTURES banner over the hallway.

We stepped under the banner and made our way toward the back doors of the school.

I could see the gray sky through the windows. The evening sun was dropping behind the hill.

"When he turns on the power," Franny said, "the voltage is so high, the whole room shakes and buzzes."

"The v-voltage?" I stammered.

"The high voltage shock usually brings most kids back," she said. "It totally revives them."

I stared hard at her. "Really?"

She slapped me on the shoulder. "Whatever it takes — right?"

We pushed open the doors and walked outside. A short staircase led down to the grass. I could see the green playing fields. Beyond the fields I saw a sloping hill.

Two boys were tossing a softball back and forth beside the baseball diamond. The ball made a nice *thud* as it hit their gloves. They weren't very good. They kept dropping the ball and having to go after it.

I didn't see anyone else outside. The sun was nearly down. The air had grown colder.

Franny and I walked toward the soccer field. The breeze blew her dark hair back, and she leaned into the wind as we walked slowly.

"So they took Wayne to the Reviver Room?" I asked. I couldn't stop thinking about it.

"He didn't come around," Franny said. She kept her eyes straight ahead.

"He's gone." She said it in a flat voice. She didn't sound upset or anything.

"Poor Angelo," I muttered. "He must be so sad."

We stepped onto the soccer field. The grass was as smooth as a golf course's.

Two huge crows cawed loudly as they flew over our heads.

I jumped, startled.

"You'll get used to the crows," Franny said. "They think they own the place."

I pointed to the tall black fence behind the soccer field. It rose up high over our heads and stretched the width of the hill.

"That fence —" I started.

"No one wants to go back there," Franny said. "Too depressing. Too sad."

34

"Huh? Sad?" I said. *What did she mean?*

Franny turned to me. "You don't want to go back there — do you, Matt?"

"No. Of course not," I said.

Little did I know that I would be *back there* before long.

And I wouldn't like it one bit!

9

The kids at Romero weren't very friendly. I mean, I found it hard to just start talking to anyone.

I'm a little bit shy. So it isn't easy for me to step into a group of strangers and start a conversation.

The kids I met in class and in the Dining Hall weren't *unfriendly*. They just didn't try very hard to talk to me. No one ever asked me where I was from or what my old school was like.

I hung out a little with Angelo. I waited for him to say something about Wayne. You know. How sad he felt or how much he missed his twin.

But he never mentioned Wayne. So I didn't, either.

We talked a lot about the soccer team and how I was going to try out for it in a few days.

And I met up with Franny a few more times. She seemed to have a lot of friends, girls mostly.

When I walked by, they'd all stop talking till I'd passed.

I wondered why they did that. But I didn't ask her.

I had a funny feeling about Franny. I always had the feeling that she was studying me. Sometimes I'd catch her eyeing me intently.

Did she think there was something *strange* about me?

One afternoon, I asked her again how long she'd been at Romero.

She tilted her head, thinking about it. "Hard to say," she replied finally.

I narrowed my eyes at her. "Huh? You don't know how long you've gone to this school?"

"Well, time gets messed up in your head," she said. "You know how it is."

I didn't know what she meant. She was always saying these mysterious things. I decided maybe *Franny* was the strange one.

A few days after I arrived, I was walking to class with Angelo. We stepped into the big round space in the middle of the school. It's called Center Court. It's a huge open space with a high dome ceiling. Above my head, a balcony stretched all around.

A large group of kids had gathered in the middle of the court. They were all gazing up at a line of kids along the balcony above.

"What's going on?" I asked Angelo. "What are they looking at?"

He didn't answer. He just pointed to the balcony.

I looked up in time to see a short, red-haired boy in dark jeans and a black T-shirt climb onto the balcony railing.

My breath caught in my throat.

What did he plan to do? Why wasn't anyone screaming or yelling for him to get down?

Behind him on the balcony, kids watched in silence. No one tried to grab him and pull him off the railing.

I froze in horror as the boy raised his hands in front of him, like he was on a diving board at a swimming pool.

He leaped off the railing, leaped high in the air — and crashed to the floor with a sick *thud.*

10

I opened my mouth to scream. But the air came out in a hoarse whisper.

I felt my knees give way. I grabbed Angelo's shoulder to keep from dropping to the floor.

The red-haired boy lay flat on his stomach, crushed to the floor, arms and legs spread out wide. He didn't move.

But no one screamed. No one rushed to help him. No one made a sound or even *moved*.

And then to my shock, kids started to cheer. I turned to Angelo and saw him clapping his hands and whistling. He pointed to the balcony again.

Another kid hoisted himself onto the narrow balcony railing. He was a big, chubby guy with short brown hair and a round red face.

"N-nooo." A low moan escaped my throat.

The kid wobbled up there for a moment. His hands flailed above his head. And then he took a flying leap.

He crashed hard to the floor with a sick *splissssh*. He bounced once. Twice. Then he didn't move.

And before I could take a breath, a girl jumped off the balcony, landed on her stomach, and collapsed in a heap beside the chubby guy.

Kids went wild, cheering and whistling and stomping their feet.

"Angelo —" I grabbed his arm and shook him. "Tell me. What's happening? This is *horrible*! Why are they cheering?"

He turned to me with a smile on his face. "One-Way Bungee Jumping," he said.

"But — but —" I sputtered.

"Hey," he said. He started to pull me to the balcony stairs. "Want to try it? Come on, Matt. Try it!"

11

A few minutes later, I called my sister on her cell. I knew she probably wouldn't believe me. But I had to tell her what happened.

"They jumped off the balcony," I said. "One by one. It was *horrible*, Jamie. They crashed to the floor. And everyone cheered. Everyone thought it was great."

Jamie laughed. I heard her shout to Mom: "It's Matt. He's still making up horror stories."

"No. Listen to me!" I cried. "I'm totally serious, Jamie. I swear. Everyone cheered when they jumped. My friend Angelo called it One-Way Bungee Jumping."

Jamie laughed even harder. "That's a riot, Matt."

"No. It was *sickening*," I insisted. "And then Angelo tried to get me to do it. Do you believe it? Luckily, the bell rang. Everyone had to get to class. And here's the weirdest part . . ."

"Your *brain* is the weirdest part," Jamie said into the phone.

"Just listen," I said. "Please. I-I'm really upset about this."

"Okay, Matt, what's the weirdest part?"

"The three kids . . . the ones who j-jumped," I stammered. "When the bell rang, they all climbed to their feet and walked away. They were perfectly okay."

Silence on the other end.

More silence.

"Jamie? Are you still there?"

"Let me get this straight," Jamie said finally. "You call me with this crazy story, right? And you expect me to believe it?"

"Yes," I said. "Because —"

"You really think I have a chimpanzee brain," Jamie said.

"No. Listen," I pleaded. "Please —"

"No. *You* listen," she said. "I like your stories, Matt. Really. They're very creative. But why can't I just listen to them? Why do I have to believe them?"

My heart was pounding hard. I knew what I'd seen was incredible. But I had to share the story. I had to make *someone* believe me.

"This school is weird," I said. "I think —"

"Gotta go," Jamie said. "Andrew is calling. Bye."

"Andrew? Who is Andrew?"

I heard a click. She was gone.

Should I call Mom or Dad?

No. Why give them a laugh? I knew they'd believe me just as much as Jamie did. And Dad would say I should be studying instead of making up horror stories.

My stomach was rumbling. I realized it was my lunch hour.

I didn't have much of an appetite. I mean, how do you eat after watching three kids go *splat* on the floor?

Sure, they got up and walked away. But in a way, that was even *more* upsetting.

I walked to the Dining Hall. I told myself to try to push the whole thing from my mind.

The big room was noisy and crowded. Chairs scraped the floor. Kids laughed and talked at the long tables. Women in white uniforms served food behind a long, steaming counter.

It seemed like a normal lunchroom — at first. But I was here my first day. I knew it wasn't like my old school.

For one thing, it was *too* noisy. I mean, the sounds weren't normal.

Kids were grunting and slurping and burping and wheezing and making loud animal sounds.

I stopped and stared at a boy at the nearest table. What was he eating? It looked like he had a slab of red, raw meat in both hands. He shoved it hungrily into his mouth. The dark juice ran down his chin.

Across from him, a girl had a huge gray blob of something. She sucked it down noisily. Then she opened her mouth in a ferocious burp.

My eyes swept over the big, crowded room. The tables were almost all filled with kids eating big chunks of red meat and hunks of blobby gray things. Raw chicken?

A boy picked up a large brown egg — shell and all — and shoved it into his mouth. Then another. Then another.

Next to him, a girl pushed a whole tomato into her mouth. Juice spurted everywhere as she closed her mouth over it. She made a loud GULP sound as she swallowed. I could *see* the entire tomato slide down her throat!

My stomach churned again.

I dreaded coming to the Dining Hall. But I *had* to eat.

I stepped up to the food counter. I saw piles of red, raw meat. Raw chicken legs. A pot of lumpy gray soup.

What could I have?

I ended up with a bunch of grapes and a bag of tortilla chips. I couldn't find anything to drink. The drink machine offered some kind of thick red juice that looked like clotted blood.

I found Angelo at a table near the back and sat down across from him. His tray was empty. He had finished his lunch.

"Can I talk to you?" I asked, scooting my chair in.

A kid at the end of the table let out a burp that shook the table. No one laughed or raised his head or acted as if it was strange.

"What's up?" Angelo asked. He had red stains on his chin.

"Well..." I didn't know how to ask about everything. I didn't want to sound stupid. But I felt so confused.

"Angelo, why is this place so weird?" I blurted out.

He gazed at me for a long time. Then he said, "You're new. You'll get used to it."

"But —" I started to ask for a better answer.

But before I could speak, a tall, dark-haired boy at the next table jumped to his feet. His eyes bulged. His mouth opened wide. And he squeezed his throat with one hand.

"UNNNNNNNNNHH!"

A horrifying groan burst from his open mouth. He wheezed. Then he let out another groan.

It took me a while to realize he was choking.

He twisted his body and grabbed at his throat.

"UNNNNNNNH."

No one moved. The kids at his table sat watching him gag and choke.

And then, the kid heaved his head back. A gigantic hunk of meat flew out of his mouth.

45

He made a gurgling sound. It seemed to come from deep in his stomach.

And then he began to spew.

Disgusting brown muck splashed from his open mouth onto the table. Gallons of it. Gallons of thick brown vomit spewed up like an erupting volcano.

"Do something!" I cried. "Somebody — *do* something!"

12

Finally, the kids at the boy's table jumped up. They stepped away from the table. But they didn't scream or call for help. Their faces were blank. As if this happened all the time.

"UNNNNNNNNH."

Another geyser of brown muck spewed over the boy's table, over everyone's food. It splashed onto the floor.

I jumped to my feet. I held my stomach. I felt like I was about to spew, too.

Still groaning and choking and vomiting, the boy staggered away from the table. He left a trail of brown muck as he stumbled out of the Dining Hall.

I turned to Angelo. He had a toothpick in his mouth and was bobbing it up and down between his lips.

"Wh-what happened?" I cried. "That boy —"

"No worries," Angelo said.

"Huh? No worries?" I shouted. "I never saw anything like that. It was *horrible*! That poor kid —"

"He'll be okay," Angelo said calmly. "He's going to the Reviver Room. You'll see. He'll be okay."

I shook my head. "Angelo, something is very wrong here. That kid definitely didn't look okay."

Later, I met Franny in the Study Room on the third floor. The room was set up like a library with bookshelves on three walls. Stretching along the fourth wall were tall windows looking down on the playing fields.

Outside the windows, a red ball of a sun was lowering itself in the evening sky. Soaring crows made a wide circle in front of the sun.

There were couches and comfortable arm-chairs to relax on and read and study. And low tables to write on or to hold a laptop.

The room was crowded. It was a popular place to go after dinner.

A sign above the door read: QUIET, PLEASE. PEOPLE STUDYING.

But I pulled Franny to a couch at the back of the room so we could talk.

She lowered her backpack to the floor and slid back on the leather couch. I dropped onto the couch beside her, eager to tell her about the kid in the Dining Hall.

48

"Matt, why are you so wired tonight?" she asked.

"Me? Wired?" I said. "How did you know?"

She rolled her eyes. "You started drumming your fingers on the couch arm as soon as we sat down. Your whole face looks like it's ready to burst. . . ."

"Okay, okay," I said. "So I'm a little wired." I raised my eyes to hers. "It's a new school, right? And there are some things about it —"

She sighed. "That again?" She slid her backpack closer. "I thought we were going to do the science worksheets together."

"Yeah. Fine. No problem," I said. "But first can we —?"

A tall, dark-haired girl from our class stepped up beside Franny. "Hey," she said. "Are you doing the worksheets?"

Franny nodded. "Yeah. If I can get Matt to get off my case."

"I'm not on your case," I said. "I just wanted to ask —"

The girl was staring down at me. She had straight black hair parted in the middle, cold blue eyes, and she wore black lipstick. "Are you the new guy?" she asked. She had a soft, whispery voice.

"That's me," I said. "I should have a T-shirt made — NEW GUY."

I thought it was funny, but she didn't laugh.

"I'm Alana," she said. She motioned for me to scoot over. "Can we do the worksheets together?"

I really wanted to talk to Franny. I had about five hundred questions about this school I needed her to answer.

But Alana was already squeezing between us. I had no choice.

We pulled out our worksheets and leaned over the table in front of the couch to fill them out together. They were long and hard. Luckily, Alana knew this chapter in the text really well. She helped Franny and me out with a lot of answers we didn't know.

I was desperate to talk to Franny alone. But every few minutes, the two of them would stop work to talk about boys in our class or some bit of gossip. Of course I had no clue of who they were talking about.

So, the study session stretched on and on. It was pitch-black outside the row of windows now. The Study Room was nearly empty.

Finally, Alana said, "Catch you guys later." She packed up her stuff and headed out the door.

I turned to Franny. "Can we talk now?" I asked eagerly. "I have some questions. . . ."

Franny jammed her worksheets into her backpack. "Can it wait till tomorrow, Matt?" she said. "I really have to get upstairs."

She didn't give me a chance to answer. She jumped to her feet.

Franny grabbed me by the shoulders. Her eyes locked on mine. "Matt — don't you realize what that means?" she cried.

I stared back at her. "No. What?"

"It means you and I are the *only living kids* in this school!" she whispered.

I blinked. My mind went blank. I couldn't think of a reply.

"You're trying to scare me?" I said finally. I grinned. "Oh, I get it. This is something kids here do to all the new students?"

"You idiot," Franny said, shaking her head. "You really haven't figured it out?"

I blinked again. I suddenly had a cold feeling at the back of my neck.

"This is a *zombie* school, Matt," Franny said. "The kids here at Romero are all undead. They are all zombies except for you and me."

She was breathing hard. She had her hands drawn into tight fists.

I finally realized she was serious. The cold feeling at the back of my neck sent a chill down my whole body.

She studied me in silence for a long moment, staring hard into my eyes. "You really are alive?"

I nodded. "I — I guess my parents didn't know what kind of school this is when they enrolled me," I stammered. "I mean, they found the school on the Internet. We didn't have time to visit here or anything."

Franny raised a finger to her lips. "*Ssshh*. It's very dangerous, Matt," she whispered. "We have to keep our secret."

"Huh? Dangerous?" My voice cracked on the words.

"We have to keep it secret that we're alive," Franny whispered. "We can't let anyone know."

"But that's . . . *crazy*," I whispered back. "If they're dead — or I mean, undead, how can we keep them from seeing that we're different?"

Franny shoved my shoulders again. "Listen to me," she said. "Listen carefully. Not too fast."

I squinted at her. "Huh?"

"Don't move too fast," she repeated. "Walk like a zombie. Stumble sometimes. Stagger to class. Bump into the wall once in a while. Don't show off by raising your hand in class. Don't try to be the first one to answer Miss Whelan's questions. You have to act like you're undead, Matt."

I stared at her, shivering from the chills rolling down my back. "You mean — I have to act like a *zombie*?"

She nodded.

"No. I can't," I whispered. "I'm out of here. I'm leaving now. I'm not even going to pack."

She squinted at me. "Escape? Do you really think you can escape this place?"

"It's pitch-black out," I said. "I can run. No one will see. I can run to the highway and then —"

Franny shook her head. "Did you see the crows outside? They're not normal crows, Matt. They're trained to guard the school grounds. You won't get ten feet before they start screeching in alarm. No one has ever escaped."

I stared hard at her, my whole body trembling. I could see she was telling the truth. There was no escape.

"So . . . I have to convince everyone I'm a zombie?" I whispered.

She nodded again. "If I can do it, you can," she said. "If they find out we're alive, they'll *kill* us!"

14

I hurtled up to my room. I grabbed my cell phone. My hand shook so hard, it took me three tries to call home.

Dad picked up on the third ring. "Hi, Matt. How's it going?"

"You — you enrolled me in a zombie school!" I blurted out.

Silence on the other end.

"Dad? Can you hear me?" My voice came out tight and shrill. "The kids at this school are all zombies!"

I heard Dad snicker. "It's Matt," he told my mom. "We put him in a school for zombies."

I heard them both laugh.

"You've got to listen to me this time. Please!" I begged.

"Talk to your mom," Dad said. "She's been really missing you."

He handed her the phone. "Hi, Matt. We were just talking about you. Really. We —"

"Mom, I'm in danger," I said. "I'm not kidding. I'm in danger."

"Well, Dad and I will be there next weekend," she said.

"Next weekend?"

"It's Parents Day," she said. "We'll be there Saturday morning. We'll take care of what's upsetting you."

"No, you won't," I said. "Saturday might be too late. This school is a zombie school, Mom. The kids are all zombies."

"Are you making any friends?" Mom asked.

I opened my mouth to answer, but I started to choke. Didn't she *hear* what I was saying? Didn't my words mean *anything* to her?

"I can't make friends, Mom," I said, sighing. "The kids are all dead. They are the living dead. Do you know what I mean?"

"Yes, I do, Matt," she replied. "You mean you are unhappy being away from home and in a new school. But you'll get used to it."

"Huh? *Used* to going to school with dead people?" I screamed.

"Please lower your voice," Mom said. "Once you make some friends, you'll feel right at home."

"I'll be dead," I said. "If I try to make friends . . ."

"Your dad wants to know if you tried out for the soccer team," Mom said.

"Tomorrow," I said. "I'm supposed to try out tomorrow, but —"

"Well, good luck. Let us know how it goes, okay?"

I sighed again. Was I getting anywhere? No. Did she hear a word I was saying? No.

"We'll see you bright and early Saturday morning," Mom said. "Bye, Matt."

"Bye." I clicked off the phone.

"Bright and early?" I muttered. "Just in time for my funeral."

A knock on my door made me jump.

"Who is it?" I called.

But the door swung open without an answer. Angelo and three other big, tough-looking boys burst into the room.

"We just found out about you," Angelo said.

15

I jumped off my bed and tried to back away. But I bumped into the dresser and nearly fell over.

"Listen, guys —" I started. "Please —"

"We just found out about you," Angelo repeated. "We just found out you were the all-star player on your old soccer team," he said.

"I — *what*?" My heart was pounding so fast, I couldn't hear what he was saying.

"Mikey here knows a guy who went to your school," Angelo said. He tapped Mikey on the chest. "That guy said you set the school records on your old team."

"Well . . . yeah," I said. I began to realize they were going to let me live. "I scored five goals in one match. But I had a lot of help. I mean, the whole team was really good."

"So you're trying out for Coach Meadows tomorrow," Angelo said.

"Yeah. Sure. Okay," I said.

"We're not giving you a choice," Mikey said. The others all laughed. "We want you on our team."

"No problem," I said.

Just don't kill me!

"Wayne didn't revive," another kid said. "So we need new flesh."

"Right. That's me," I said. *New flesh.* "See you tomorrow after class."

They turned and marched out.

I stood there trembling. Was I going to be the next great zombie soccer star?

"Matt, go in and play forward," Coach Meadows said. He didn't look like a coach at all. He was bald and had a thin, saggy face with droopy eyes and drooping cheeks.

He was skinny as a broomstick and a little stooped over. The whistle around his neck hung down to the waist of his gray sweatsuit.

"I know you can kick," he said. "I want to see good offense, too."

He motioned me into the practice game. Two teams — one in black, one in red — were already warming up.

I pulled on a red sweatshirt and jogged onto the field. We lined up, and Coach Meadows blew the whistle to start the match.

The red team kicked off to the black. The kick didn't go far. A black-shirt player kicked it upfield to a teammate. They kicked it back and forth to each other, running toward our goal.

But they moved so slowly, I jumped in front of them and stole the ball. I dribbled it between my feet, then passed off to Angelo in the corner of the field.

My kick was too hard. Angelo couldn't get to it, and the ball bounced off the field.

Angelo tossed the ball inbounds. The other players lurched toward it. But I got there first. I dribbled it halfway down the field.

I looked for someone to pass it to. But the players on both teams were far behind me. I was all alone with the goal in front of me.

That's when I glimpsed the sidelines — and saw that everyone was staring at me. Staring hard.

At first, I thought it was because I was playing so well.

But then I remembered Franny's warning — and I knew why they were watching me with such unpleasant looks on their faces.

Don't move too fast. Walk like a zombie.

That was Franny's advice. And here I was, showing off my skills. Showing off how fast I was.

I was so much faster than the other players, they were starting to suspect me. Starting to suspect that I was *alive*.

I deliberately stumbled. I let the ball roll away from me. And I fell facedown onto the grass.

A black-shirt player caught up to the ball and began moving it the other way.

I pulled myself to my feet slowly. I turned and started toward the ball.

Slow down, Matt, I told myself. *Take slow, lurching steps.*

The other players were all moving in slow motion. And now so was I.

I glanced at the sidelines. Coach Meadows had a smile on his droopy face.

I was fooling him. I was fooling everyone.

Slow . . . slow . . .

The ball was loose. I moved in to kick it downfield.

I gave a hard kick. I saw the red-shirt player in front of me. Saw his mouth open in surprise.

I didn't mean to kick him. But my shoe slammed hard into his leg.

I heard a sick *craaaack*.

The boy uttered a gasp as his leg cracked.

And then I screamed as the whole leg came flying off.

16

The leg bounced to the grass. The boy's sneaker made a soft *thud* as it landed. The leg lay flat on the field.

The boy stood there on one leg, gazing down at it. His eyes were wide with shock. "I : . . don't . . . believe it," he murmured.

My stomach lurched. I spun away. Dropped to my knees. Covered my face with my hands.

"Oh, noooo," I moaned. "What have I done?"

I stayed down on the ground with my face covered for a long time. I wanted it all to go away. Everything. This horrible school. These frightening kids.

When I looked up, the boy was being carried away on a stretcher. He was on his back, and he held the leg up high in one hand. He waved it at the sky like a trophy.

I felt sick. I struggled to keep my lunch down. The ground spun in front of me.

I realized someone had a hand on my shoulder. I gazed up to see Coach Meadows beside me.

His face seemed to sag even more. His eyes were sad. He reached out his hands. "Stand up, Matt," he said.

He helped pull me to my feet. My legs were shaky. I thought I might fall right back down.

I pictured that leg lying on the grass.

No blood. The leg cracked off, but the boy didn't bleed.

"Don't worry, Matt," the coach said softly. "Stop thinking about it. It wasn't your fault."

"But —" I started. My words caught in my throat.

"These injuries happen all the time," Coach Meadows said.

"They do?" I choked out.

He nodded solemnly. Behind him, the other players stared at me blankly. They didn't react at all to a guy losing his whole leg!

"You looked pretty good out there," the coach said. He rubbed his bald head. "Actually, you looked *very* good."

Until I kicked a player's leg off.

"Let's call it for today," Coach Meadows said. "Go to your room, Matt, and don't think about soccer. They took Davey to the Reviver Room. He'll be back in time for practice tomorrow."

"He will?" I said. "Oh. Uh . . . good." I didn't want to act too surprised. I had to act like the other players.

Coach Meadows blew his whistle. His whole body sagged, as if it took all his strength to make it work.

"Tomorrow at four!" he announced to everyone. He flashed me a thumbs-up and slumped toward the back of the school.

Most of the players started to jog up the hill with the coach. I walked slowly after them.

But Angelo and his friend Mikey stepped up to block my way. They both eyed me suspiciously.

"You're just nervous — right?" Angelo said.

"Uh . . . yeah. I'm kind of nervous," I replied.

Mikey scowled at me. "You're tense and pumped up," he said. "That's why you ran so much faster than us?"

I swallowed hard. My mouth suddenly felt dry as cotton.

I didn't want to be caught. Saturday was Parents Day. Maybe my parents could get me away from here before the zombie kids realized I wasn't one of them.

I just had to be careful. Very, very careful.

"Uh, yeah," I said. "Whenever I'm really pumped, I act like that. You know. Almost like I'm alive. But I'm not. I'm still dead, see. I mean, still undead. Whatever. Really."

That didn't come out right.

The two big hulks didn't move. They continued to study me, their faces frozen with scowls.

Mikey motioned to the field. "You were very fast," he said.

"Just nerves," I said.

Angelo squinted at me. "Dude, when did you die?" he asked.

"Recently," I said. "Very recently."

They both nodded.

"Catch you later," Mikey said.

They both jogged off toward the school.

I stood there shaking. I realized I had sweat pouring down my face.

This is what REAL horror is like, I told myself.

I swore to myself if I survived this school, I'd never go to another horror movie.

I just had to make it till Saturday. Saturday morning, my parents would arrive. Could I convince them to take me away from here?

Could I convince them to save my life?

17

Saturday morning, I woke up early. I skipped breakfast and waited at the front of the school for Mom and Dad to arrive.

It was a gray morning with dark clouds low overhead. From time to time, lightning flashed in the black clouds. Thunder rumbled far in the distance.

Perfect for a horror movie.

In my head, I kept running over and over all the things I wanted to tell my parents. I knew it would be hard to make them believe my story.

So I knew I had to *show* them I was telling the truth. I planned to give them a tour of the school that would convince them beyond a doubt that we were surrounded by zombies.

The night before, I'd looked for Franny. I wanted to ask if her parents were coming, too. I wanted to ask if she was as desperate to get out of this zombie school as I was.

But she was studying with a group of girls. And I didn't get to talk to her.

I paced back and forth in the front hall. Most kids were still in the Dining Hall having their breakfast.

Finally, I saw my parents' car curling up the long driveway. I shoved open the doors and rushed out to meet them.

A light rain had started to fall. By the time my dad parked the car, I was fairly soaked.

But I didn't care. It was *Escape Time*.

First, we had a lot of hugs. My parents kept saying how much they missed me, even though it had only been two weeks.

"Jamie misses you, too," Mom said. "But she'd never admit it."

"Where *is* Jamie?" I asked.

"She had too much homework. She had to stay home," Mom said. "She's in high school, you know. They give a lot of homework."

I sighed. "Here, too."

We started to walk to the front entrance. "How's school going?" Dad asked. "Better than the last time you called?"

"No," I said. I stopped them on the front walk. "I really need you to listen to me. I need you to believe me. Everything I've told you about this school — I'm not making it up."

They both groaned. "Please, Matt. Don't start with that zombie nonsense," Dad said. "Let's have a nice day together and talk about *real* things."

"Wait. Wait," I said. I blocked their path to the front doors. "Let's make a deal," I said. "Just give me a chance to prove my case. Okay? I mean, just keep an open mind."

"But how can we —?" Dad started.

I put my hands together like I was begging. "Just let me take you around this morning," I said. "Let me show you some things and let you talk to some kids. That's all. Just don't make up your minds till after lunch. Is that okay?"

They exchanged glances. "This is crazy," Mom muttered. "You're keeping us out here in the rain. For what? You really want us to believe there are zombies in this school?"

"I'm going to show you," I said. "If you'll give me a chance."

Silence for a long moment. "Okay," Dad said finally. "Deal."

"And then you'll drop the whole zombie nonsense?" Mom asked.

"Open mind," I said. "Remember? You're keeping an open mind?"

I turned to the school entrance. I saw the principal, Mr. Craven, step out to the top of the stairs. A flash of lightning made his bald onion head glow.

I turned back to Mom and Dad. "Okay," I said. "There's Mr. Craven. Remember him? Get ready. Here's your first clue."

18

Rain pattered on the walk as we made our way to the front steps. Mr. Craven had a big smile on his round, pale face. He had his hands in the jacket pockets of the baggy gray suit he wore every day.

I knew he was eager to give Mom and Dad a big greeting.

"Now be sure to shake hands with him," I told them. "He's a zombie, so his hands will be ice-cold. Dry and cold. That's because he's dead."

Mom frowned at me. "The man probably has bad circulation."

"Yes. Very bad circulation," I said. "Because he's *dead*!"

"*Ssshh*. He'll hear you," Mom whispered.

I heard a clatter of shoes on the walk. I turned to see a big black umbrella. A man and a woman were hunched under it, jogging quickly toward us.

Visiting parents.

They passed us and climbed the stairs to Mr. Craven. Craven's smile grew wider. He greeted them warmly and shook their hands. He waved them into the building.

We were right behind them. "Get ready," I whispered.

"Hello, Krinskys," Craven said warmly. "Hurry. Get out of the rain." He held the door open and waved us inside.

Mom and Dad started into the school. "No — wait," I said. "Shake hands. Shake his hand."

Too late. We were inside.

The other parents closed their umbrella and shook it out. Mom and Dad wiped rainwater from their hair. Two more parents burst in behind us.

"Mom, Dad — don't you see how pale the other parents are?" I asked.

They frowned. "It's a dark, rainy day, Matt," Dad said. "Everyone looks pale."

"Welcome, everyone. Welcome," Craven gushed, ignoring the raindrops running down his bald head.

"He seems perfectly nice," Mom whispered.

"You are welcome to wander around the school," Craven announced. "It is Saturday, so our students will be relaxed and casual."

"They're so relaxed, they're *dead*," I whispered.

Mom shushed me and gazed at the zombie principal.

"If you are hungry from your trip, breakfast

is still being served in the Dining Hall," Craven said.

"Yes! Breakfast!" I cried. I wanted my parents to see the disgusting stuff these undead kids ate. And the gross, sickening way they ate it.

"Come on," I said, pulling them by the hand. "Breakfast. You have to see this."

"I don't think so," Mom said. "We had a big breakfast before we left."

"Let's just wander around a bit," Dad said. "Show us what you've done to your room."

"No. Breakfast," I insisted. "You don't have to eat. I just want you to see it."

They both shrugged. I led the way upstairs. I knew when they saw the zombie kids eating, they'd *have* to believe me.

As soon as we reached the second floor, I could smell the food. For breakfast, the cooks serve huge vats of nearly raw eggs, pots of bacon fat, big gray pancakes that tasted like dirt, and fruit plates piled up with brown fruits that must have decayed ten years ago.

The zombie kids lap it up. I usually had a bowl of Frosted Flakes with milk — unless they were serving sour milk that day. Then, I ate the cereal with orange juice.

"Mmmmm. Smells good," Dad said, sniffing the air. "Reminds me of *my* school days."

"It won't," I said. I pushed open the double doors for them. "Come on in. See how zombies eat."

I led them inside. I glanced around. Perfect. At the first table, a boy was shoving raw eggs into his mouth with both hands. He had egg yolk all over his face.

Near the back, some guys were tossing a gray pancake back and forth like a Frisbee. Two girls were shoving black sausages into their mouths as fast as they could.

I turned to Mom and Dad. They were watching the whole thing with shocked expressions on their faces.

"See?" I said eagerly. "See?"

Then they both started laughing.

"Nothing ever changes," Mom said.

Dad shook his head. "We were much worse," he said. "Wow. I remember the incredible food fights we used to have. The whole lunchroom would be covered in slop."

"Kids will always be kids," Mom said. "Just look at them."

"But — but — but —" I sputtered. "Don't you see? These aren't normal kids. They —"

"Of course they are," Dad said. He tugged my arm and guided me to the doors. "What could be more normal? Come on. Let's go. Mom and I want to see your room."

"Take us around the school. Give us the full tour," Mom said.

I sighed. So far, I was a total failure. How could I convince them they were in a zombie school?

This was my only chance to prove I wasn't making up a horror story. I had to convince them. My life depended on it.

I led them upstairs past the Study Room. Through the glass door, I could see zombie kids studying in there, tapping away on their laptops.

Angelo wandered past. He waved and called out my name.

"A new friend?" Mom asked.

"He's on the soccer team," I said. "But if he finds out I'm alive, he'll probably kill me."

The bell rang overhead just as I said that. Mom and Dad didn't hear me.

"I like the calm atmosphere here," Dad said. "Everyone moves so slowly. No one is in a hurry. It's a very relaxed place."

"Dad, they're moving slowly because they're undead," I said. "That's as fast as they can move."

They both laughed.

"You're not convincing us," Mom said. She glanced at her watch. "You don't have much time left to show us your proof."

"I know," I said.

We stepped into the Center Court in the middle of the school. I looked up at the balcony. And suddenly I knew.

I knew I was going to convince my parents this was a zombie school.

They were about to see the proof with their own eyes.

19

A few kids gathered in the court. They moved in front of us. They all had their eyes on the balcony.

A few seconds later, a girl peered over the railing. She had short blond hair tied in pigtails. She wore a black sweater over black jeans.

"Watch," I told my parents. I motioned to the balcony. "Just watch this. It's going to be horrible. But maybe you'll believe me."

The girl started to pull herself up to the top of the balcony wall.

"Oh. Hey," Dad said. He fumbled in his pants pocket. He pulled out his phone. "Oh. Sorry. I have a call."

He started to raise the phone to his ear. But it slipped out of his hand.

The phone hit the hard floor with a *clang*.

The blond-haired girl leaped off the balcony and hit the floor. She thudded heavily, and she bounced twice before landing in a heap.

"Did you see —?" I started. Then I gasped.

Both of my parents had their backs turned. They were both bending over to pick up Dad's phone.

"I'll bet it was Jamie," Dad said. He grabbed the phone and studied it.

"Is it okay? Did it break?" Mom asked.

"Didn't you see her jump!" I screamed. *"Didn't you see what just happened?"*

Dad squinted at the phone screen. "It seems to be okay," he said.

"Check the call log," Mom said. "Was that Jamie calling?"

I totally lost it. I started screaming my head off. "That girl jumped off the balcony!" I cried. "Didn't you see her?"

Kids turned to look at me. I realized it was dangerous to scream.

"Where?" Mom asked. "Who jumped? Where?"

I pointed. The blond-haired girl was climbing to her feet. She brushed off the front of her sweater. She started to walk away.

"She couldn't have jumped," Mom said. "Look. She's walking away. Why would you say such a crazy thing?"

"Matt, it's time to drop the whole zombie thing," Dad said. "We gave you a chance. Now it's just getting tired."

I failed again. Failed. Failed. Failed.

I wanted to jump up and down and scream and throw myself into the wall and — and —

Wait. One last try. One last chance to save my life.

I knew who could help me. I knew who could convince them.

My parents wouldn't listen to me. But they *would* listen to Franny.

Franny. The only other living kid in this school.

Franny would tell them this is a zombie school. And they would believe her.

Now where could I find her? She could be anywhere.

And then I nearly cried out when I saw Franny step into the court. She wore a red-and-black Romero sweatshirt over a short black skirt. She had a bulging backpack on her shoulders.

I guessed she was headed to the Study Room upstairs.

"Franny! Hey!" I took off, running through the crowded circle of kids. "Franny!"

She turned and waited for me. "Matt, what's up?"

"Did your parents come?" I asked.

She shook her head. "Not this time. Yours?"

"Yes," I said. "I want you to meet them. I want you to tell them —"

"Tell them?" Franny said.

I turned. My parents had followed me across

the hall. Dad was texting someone on his phone. Mom smiled at Franny.

"This is Franny. She's in my class," I said.

Mom and Dad said hi. Dad frowned at the phone and tucked it into his pants pocket.

"Have you been at Romero long?" Mom asked her.

"This is my second year," Franny said. She shifted her backpack on her shoulders.

"I've been trying to tell my mom and dad about this school," I told Franny. "But they don't believe me."

She giggled. "Really?"

Dad rolled his eyes. "You're not starting this stuff again, are you? In front of your friend?"

"Tell them," I said to Franny. "Go ahead. Tell them the truth about this school. They won't believe me — but they'll believe you."

Franny squinted at me. "The truth?"

"Yes," I insisted. "Go ahead. Tell them what's *special* about this school."

Franny raised her eyes to the ceiling, as if she was thinking hard. She took a deep breath. Finally, she started. "Well . . ."

20

"I guess the *library* is really special," Franny said. "It's open twenty-four hours a day, and they have thousands of books. And tons of computers with a very fast connection."

"That's nice," Mom said with a smile.

"And the Dining Hall is pretty special," Franny added.

I groaned. "Franny, you know that's not what I meant." My heart was pounding. I wanted to explode. Why was she *doing* this?

"Tell my parents about the zombies!" I screamed.

Several kids turned to stare at me.

Franny scrunched up her face. "Zombies?"

"Tell them what you told me," I begged. "You know. That this is a zombie school. That you and I are the only *living* kids here."

Franny laughed. "Matt, tell me you didn't believe me," she said. "I was joking. You know. A joke for the new kid in school."

Dad slapped my shoulder. "Guess we won't be hearing about *that* anymore," he said. "Thank you, Franny."

"But — but —" I sputtered.

Franny turned to the door. "I have to go study," she said. She grinned. "You know. Meet up with the other zombies and maybe rip some live flesh while we do our math."

Mom and Dad laughed.

I could feel my face go red-hot. I mean, my blood was *boiling*.

Franny took a few steps, then turned back. "Matt, are you coming to the dance party after all the parents leave tonight?" she called.

"Party?" I could barely get the word out. I felt so angry and upset, I was shaking. "I don't think so," I replied.

Franny waved good-bye to my parents. Then she hurried away.

"You should go to the party," Mom said. "You've got to stop living in your own world, Matt."

I didn't answer. My head was still burning hot. My hands were balled into tight fists.

"You've got to make friends here and try to fit in," Dad said.

Fit in? That's a laugh. Fit in with a school full of zombies. For sure.

"Franny seems nice," Mom said.

Nice? She's a liar and a traitor, I thought.

She was my last chance. And now I was doomed. Trapped in this school with the living dead. Trapped here — until the kids discovered I was alive. And then they'd make me undead, too.

"What are you thinking about?" Mom asked.

I shrugged. "I'm thinking I should show you my room. I made it very cool," I said.

I tried to act "normal" for the rest of the day. I didn't mention zombies. How could I?

Parents Day was one of the longest days of my life. I couldn't really talk to my parents at all. I just kept thinking about how I was DOOMED.

Finally, that evening, I said good-bye to Mom and Dad on the front steps of the school. I promised I would go to the dance party and tell them all about it.

Then I hugged them and watched them walk to their car. A wave of sadness rolled over me. I knew it would probably be the last time I ever saw them.

I didn't want to go to any party. I wanted to run to my room, lock the door, and hide under the bed.

But before I could do that, I had to find Franny. I had to find out why she lied to my parents. Why she refused to save my life.

I found her upstairs in her room. She and her roommate, Marcia, were in front of the mirror, doing each other's hair, getting ready for the party.

I barged in without knocking. "Why?" I demanded. My voice came out higher and shriller than I'd planned. "Why? Just tell me why!"

Both girls turned to me.

"What's your problem?" Marcia asked.

"I'm not talking to you," I said. "Franny knows what I'm talking about." I put my hands on my hips and waited for Franny to answer me.

She turned to Marcia. "He's the new kid and he has issues," she said.

Marcia made a face. "Issues? What does that mean?"

"He's crazy," Franny replied.

She tugged me out into the hall. A lot of kids were already heading to the party in the gym. She pulled me into an empty room.

"Matt, are you totally losing it?" she said in a harsh whisper.

"Why didn't you tell my parents the truth?" I demanded. "Why didn't you tell them this is a zombie school, and you and I are the only living kids?"

She put a finger on my lips to hush me up.

"I want to *stay* alive. That's why," she said. "Matt, there were at least a dozen kids listening to us talk to your parents this morning. Didn't you see them?"

"No," I said. "I —"

"I couldn't talk in that crowd," Franny said. "I couldn't tell your parents the truth. If I did, we'd both be undead by now. I'm serious."

I stared at her. "You could have saved my life."

She shook her head. "No way. Those kids were listening, Matt. They wouldn't let you leave the school with your parents. They would have gotten to you before you stepped out the door."

I opened my mouth to speak but no words came to me.

"They are watching you, Matt," Franny said. "I think they are starting to suspect."

That sent a chill to the back of my neck.

"You don't understand how much danger you are in," she said.

"You're not cheering me up," I said.

It was kind of a joke, but she didn't laugh. "Just be careful," she said. "Listen to me. At the party tonight, be very careful."

If only I had listened to her . . .

21

My parents told me to go to the party and *try to fit in*. What a joke.

I didn't want to fit in with the kids in this school. I kind of wanted to be *alive*.

But Franny convinced me I had to go. She said if I didn't go to the party, kids would wonder why I wanted to be different.

"I can do this," I told myself. I figured if Franny could play dead and fool everyone, I could, too.

I pulled on a fairly clean pair of faded cargo jeans and a black pullover shirt. Then I pawed through my horror collection.

I was looking for something the other kids might think was funny. You know. Something to convince these zombies that I was a good guy.

I pulled out the perfect thing. A human hand. Actually, it was made of rubber. But it looked very real.

I turned it over in my hands a few times. I decided I could probably make kids laugh with it. So I tucked it into my jeans pocket and headed to the gym for my first party at Romero.

I don't know what I expected. Maybe black crepe streamers on the ceiling. Black candles. Gravestones for decoration. Music by the Grateful Dead.

I pushed open the gym doors and gazed inside. It looked like a normal party.

Red balloons bobbed overhead. Kids hung out around a long food table against one wall. Some kids sat in the bleachers, talking and laughing.

A few girls danced together to loud music in the center of the floor. Some boys leaned against the wall, watching them.

I strode quickly across the floor — then stopped. I remembered what Franny had said. *Not too fast.*

I took a few lurching steps. I pretended to stumble. Then I staggered toward the food table.

I could see kids in the bleachers watching me. I hoped my zombie walk looked real to them.

Slow, Matt. Keep it slow.

I waved to Marcia, Franny's roommate. She stared back at me. I don't think she liked me. Maybe she suspected I didn't belong in this school.

I wondered if she suspected Franny, too.

I spotted Angelo and Mikey and some of the other soccer players at the food table. They held big hunks of red meat in their hands. They were stuffing their faces, gobbling and swallowing so loudly, I could hear them above the pounding music.

I lurched toward them, remembering to stagger and stumble. I was halfway across the gym floor when Mikey suddenly erupted.

A hoarse honking sound burst from his throat like a blast from a tuba. His eyes went wide. He grabbed his throat with both hands.

Mikey staggered crazily over the floor, making frightening honking, bleating sounds. It took me a few seconds to realize he was choking on a big hunk of raw meat.

Angelo stepped up behind Mikey and pounded him hard on the back.

Mikey made a sickening ULLLLLP sound.

Angelo pounded his back again. A few kids gasped as Mikey's big pink tongue came flying out.

The tongue sailed several feet. Then it hit the gym floor and bounced once or twice.

I gaped at it in horror. My stomach tightened into a knot.

The tongue was *moving*!

It wiggled on the hardwood floor.

No one screamed. No one made a sound.

Mikey stopped choking. He bent down and

picked up his tongue in one hand. Then he hurried out of the gym, carrying it carefully in front of him.

I made my way to Angelo. "Mikey's tongue —" I choked out. I couldn't keep the alarm from my voice.

Angelo waved his hand. "He'll be okay," he said. "He does that all the time."

My stomach was doing flip-flops. I kept picturing the tongue wiggling all by itself on the gym floor. But I tried to act normal.

Angelo offered me a huge chunk of red meat. "Snack?" he asked.

It smelled rotten. I forced myself not to make a disgusted face or back away.

"No, thanks," I said. "I had that for dinner."

He blinked at me. "You coming to practice Monday?"

I nodded. "For sure."

Angelo grinned and pumped his fist in the air. "The Vultures are going to *kill* this year!" he cried. "Kill, kill, KILL!"

"Yeah. Kill," I repeated.

The music changed. Some kids shouted: "Time for the Stomp! Everyone! Do the Stomp!"

I watched in surprise as everyone formed a line across the gym floor. The music pounded, and everyone started a weird, stomping dance.

Two girls I didn't know pulled me into the line. They stomped their feet, then shuffled to one side. Then they stomped some more and slid the other way.

Everyone in the gym seemed to know this dance. Everyone but *me*.

I struggled to catch on quickly.

Stomp stomp stompstompstomp slide.

Stomp stomp stompstompstomp slide.

"Ohhh," I cried out as I fell into the girl next to me. We both nearly hit the floor.

Another girl pulled me back up. I tried again. Everyone was doing it. Everyone was dancing and stomping and having a great time.

Stomp stomp stompstompstomp slide.

"Owww." I slid onto my own shoe and tripped. I hit the floor. Banged my knees hard.

The music stopped. I was still on my knees.

A heavy silence fell over the gym. I turned to see everyone staring at me.

Slowly, I climbed to my feet. "I'm such a total klutz," I said. "I . . . uh . . . I'm usually great at the Stomp. It's my favorite."

Four grim-faced boys came marching toward me. They squinted at me menacingly.

I turned to run. But some kids moved to block the gym doors.

The four boys lurched up to me, hands on their waists. They didn't blink. They stared hard, as if studying me.

A chill ran down my back. "What's the problem?" I asked in a tiny voice.

22

I'd seen these guys in the halls. They always walked together, kind of strutting. They waved and called out to everyone they passed.

They were popular. They seemed to know everyone.

All four of them were dressed in dark khaki cargo pants and black shirts that came down nearly to their knees. Like they were in a club or something.

They were pretty okay looking for zombies. Tall and athletic. Three blond dudes and one with red hair. The red-haired guy had a black patch over one eye.

Their skin was very pale and tight on their faces. Otherwise, they could pass for normal living kids.

They formed a semicircle around me. They grinned at me, but their eyes were cold.

"I'm Ernie," one of them said. "How you doing?"

"F-fine," I stuttered. "Good party."

"You like it here?" he asked. He seemed to be the spokesman. The other three had their grins frozen on their faces, like they were wearing masks.

"Yeah. Good school," I said.

Ernie looked me up and down. "You *sure* you like it here?"

"Yeah. Sure," I said. My legs were shaking like they were made of Jell-O.

"Hard being the new kid, huh?" Ernie said. The other three boys snickered.

I swallowed. "Yeah. But everyone's been totally nice," I said. My voice cracked on the word *nice.*

Ernie's grin turned into a sneer. "You're not too good at the Stomp," he said. He swung around to his friends. "Not too good, is he?"

"Not too good," the red-haired dude chimed in.

"Maybe he needs to practice," another guy said. "You know. With us."

"Yeah. Maybe he needs to practice," Ernie agreed. "What do *you* think, Matt? Think you need to practice?"

"Well . . . uh . . ."

Before I could answer, Franny appeared. She pushed her way into the center of the group. "What's up, guys?" she asked.

"We were just making friends," Ernie replied. "Trying to help out the new kid."

"Yeah. Making friends," the red-haired guy repeated. His expression didn't look too friendly.

"Come on, Ernie. This is a party," Franny said. She pulled me away. "Give Matt a break. Why do you want to get up in his face?"

Ernie threw his hands up. "Just making friends," he said. The other three laughed.

Franny dragged me away. "Those guys are dangerous," she whispered.

The music started up again. Everyone started talking at once, as if someone had pushed an ON button.

Franny pulled me behind the bleachers. A food fight had broken out above us in the seats. Kids were heaving blobs of meat and rotten fruit at one another. The bleachers shook from all the commotion.

"Those guys are really popular," Franny said. "They rule the school."

"They weren't being friendly," I said. "They lied about that."

"They suspect you," Franny said. "They think you're alive."

"I *am* alive," I said. "We're both alive, right? How come they don't pick on *you*?"

"Because I'm a better actor than you," she said.

Loud cheers rang out above us. The bleachers shook. A fat blob of meat came sailing down and squished at my feet.

"I'm going to help you," Franny said. "Here's what we're going to do. First, you're going to dance with me. Dance like a zombie. Everyone will be watching you."

"Nice. No pressure," I said.

"Don't make jokes. Your life depends on this," Franny said, frowning. "After our dance, go over to the food table. Convince everyone there that you're one of them."

I gulped. "You mean —?"

A new song started. Another stomping beat. Franny pulled me out onto the floor.

A lot of kids were dancing now. Strange, stiff-legged dancing, as if their knees didn't bend.

"You can do it. Just copy them," Franny said.

We started to dance. I kept my knees stiff. I bumped into Franny a few times.

"Good!" she said. "Keep it up."

We danced a bit harder. I stumbled around in a circle.

"Good!" Franny urged me on. "Now stagger right into the wall."

I followed her instruction. I staggered into the wall. Then I shuffled back to her.

"Franny," I said. I had my eyes on the bleachers. "Ernie and his friends — they're still watching me."

"Of course they are," she replied. "Listen, Matt, I'll help you as much as I can. But you have to do everything you can to make them think you are undead."

"Everything?" I asked.

Franny gave me a shove. "To the food table. Now. Put on a good show, Matt. After a while, they'll stop watching you."

I had no choice. I staggered over to the food table. I saw a swarm of flies buzzing over the decayed fruit and plates of raw meat. Some of the meat had turned green.

I held my breath to keep the putrid smell from my nose. I gazed down the table, searching for something I could possibly eat.

No way.

A tall, black-haired girl in a short purple skirt and purple sweater tapped me on the shoulder.

Startled, I spun around. "Oh. Hi."

"I'm Evie," she said. "Here. Have you tried this? It's just ripe enough."

She picked up a blob of green, rotting meat and dangled it in front of my eyes.

I tried not to make a face, but I couldn't help it.

She laughed. "Go ahead. Try it."

"I . . . don't think so," I said. I saw Franny watching me from the dance floor. I knew I had to do as Franny said. I had to convince Evie I was a zombie like her.

But *no way* could I eat that putrid raw meat.

I grabbed a rotted pear from the bowl. "I . . . I like fruit," I told her. "Have you tried the pears?"

"I've had six of them," she said. "They're awesome."

Evie waited for me to eat the pear. I gazed at it, and I nearly heaved.

The skin had rotted off, and the fruit inside was spotty brown with green stuff growing on it. It was covered in deep wormholes.

"Yummmm," I said.

I can't do this, I thought. *I'm going to heave. I really am.*

Evie didn't move. Her eyes were on the pear. I turned and glimpsed Ernie and his three friends at the other end of the food table. They were watching me, too.

I took a deep, shuddering breath. And held it.

Then slowly ... slowly, I raised the rotted, wormy pear to my mouth.

Every muscle in my body tightened as I opened my mouth — and shoved the pear inside.

It felt dry and lumpy against my tongue. Like a dead frog. That's what I suddenly pictured — a dead frog.

I couldn't chew it. My stomach was heaving ... heaving.

I ... swallowed it whole!

My whole body shook. I swallowed again ... again. I knew I'd never get that bitter, rancid taste from my mouth. Never.

Evie smiled at me. "Good, huh? Try another one."

"Uh ... no," I said. My mind was spinning.

How could I get away from this horrifying food table?

"Want to dance?" I asked.

She nodded. "Sure."

She took my hand. She started to lead me to the other dancers.

Her hand was ice-cold. The cold made my whole arm tingle.

Suddenly, she stopped. Her smile faded. She let go of my hand. Her eyes went wide.

"Oh, Matt, nooooo," she moaned.

Then she turned to the other kids and started to scream at the top of her lungs:

"Hey! He's still warm! Hey, everyone — he's still WARM!"

23

I uttered a cry. I wanted to run.

But Evie grabbed my hand with both of hers and held on. "It's warm! It's WARM!" she screamed.

I tried to pull myself free. But she had surprising strength. I realized there was nowhere to run anyway.

The music stopped. A crowd of kids gathered around Evie and me. Ernie and his friends pushed them out of the way to get to me. Evie let go of my hand and backed away.

My mind spun. How was I going to get out of this one? I searched the crowd for Franny. But the faces were a blur. I couldn't find her.

Ernie stepped up inches from my face. He gazed hard into my eyes. "Matt, when did you die?" he demanded.

Think fast, Matt. Think fast.

"Uh . . . last Sunday," I said.

Ernie narrowed his eyes at me. "That can't be right," he said. "I remember you arrived here at school two Sundays ago."

Panic gripped my throat. I could barely choke out a sound.

"Uh . . . let's see," I rasped. "I guess . . . I died two weeks ago. No. Three. I remember it was a Tuesday."

This was *not* going well.

The huge gym grew silent. The air suddenly felt steamy and hot. I had sweat pouring down my face.

Again, I searched for Franny. No sight of her. Besides, what could she do to help me? She had to keep *her* secret safe.

Ernie leaned over me. I could smell the rotted meat on his breath. "This is a special school," he said. "I think you know what I mean by *special.*"

"Yeah. Of course," I choked out.

"And we don't want outsiders to find out about our school," he said. "They might decide to cause trouble."

"No. N-no trouble," I stammered.

I gazed over his big shoulders to the gym doors. No way I'd ever make it. I was trapped.

"Test him!" a boy cried from the crowd. "Give him the test."

I turned and saw that it was Angelo. Some friend!

97

"Test him! Test him! Test him!" Some kids took up the chant.

Ernie grabbed my shoulders and spun me around. He pushed me toward the gym doors.

"Where are you taking me?" I cried.

Panic made my legs quiver like rubber bands. I nearly collapsed to the floor. But Ernie held on to me.

"What are you going to do?"

"This way," Ernie ordered. He pushed open the doors and shoved me out into the hall.

"Test him! Test him! Test him!" The chanting zombie kids came following close behind us.

"Uh . . . could I take a makeup test?" I said. "Maybe next week?"

My words were drowned out by the loud chant of the excited kids. Their cries rang off the tile walls as we marched down the halls.

The long halls twisted and turned. The school was built in circles. As we followed the halls around, I totally lost my direction. In my panic, it all became a frightening blur of empty rooms and gray lockers and dimly lit hallways.

Until we stepped into the Center Court.

Then everything snapped back into focus. The wide, round, open space in the center of the school. The domed ceiling. The balcony circling the court, high above.

Yes, I knew where I was now.

I felt Ernie's hands on my shoulders as he

guided me from behind. Guided me up the long, steep stairway that led to the balcony.

"Nooooo. Please —"

Was that *me* pleading in that high, trembling voice?

Yes, it was.

I didn't want to climb up to the balcony. I didn't want to be up there. Because I could guess what was about to happen.

The noisy, excited crowd of kids stayed down below. And now a *new* chant rose up: "Bungee jump! Bungee jump! Bungee jump!"

The words rang in my ears until my head felt about to explode. I knew. I knew what my test would be. The test that would definitely show if I was alive or undead.

Ernie pushed me to the balcony railing. I gazed down. The kids filled the court, all eyes raised to me. Chanting . . . chanting.

The floor was a mile down. And solid marble.

I knew I couldn't survive a jump. When I hit, I'd break every bone in my body.

"What are you waiting for?" Ernie demanded, giving me another push.

"Well . . . I have a problem with heights," I said.

"Get up on the railing," he ordered. "Go ahead. It's easy. Once you pass the test, I'll get out of your face. Promise."

Pass the test?

How could I pass the test?

I glanced down again. Big mistake. The sight of the hard marble floor so far below me made my whole body shudder.

I shut my eyes. I pictured an egg falling from high up. *Craaaack. Splaaaaat.*

I tried to back away from the balcony edge. But Ernie stood right behind me. I couldn't move an inch.

"Bungee jump! Bungee jump!" The cry rose up from the kids down below.

I wrapped both hands on the balcony railing and pulled myself up.

Were these my final seconds of being alive?

What could I possibly do to save myself?

Nothing.

I shut my eyes. I thought: *Good-bye, Mom and Dad. Good-bye, Jamie.*

Good-bye, everyone.

24

Then I remembered the fake rubber hand.

I had tucked it into a pocket of my cargo jeans. Could that rubber hand save my life? I suddenly had an idea.

I twisted my body so that Ernie couldn't see what I was doing. Then I pulled the hand out from my pocket.

Gripping it tightly in my right hand, I pulled the rubber hand into my shirtsleeve.

I leaned over the balcony.

The chanting stopped. The kids grew silent. Everyone froze.

I leaned a little farther over the edge. I could see the eyes all raised to me. See the eager looks on all the faces.

I leaned even farther. Stretched my hands over the side. And dropped the rubber hand from my shirtsleeve.

Kids gasped as it fell. It hit the floor hard and

bounced two or three times. It rolled into a corner beneath the balcony and stopped.

"My hand!" I screamed. "My hand! That's the *third* time! I can't keep it on!"

Silence down below. An eerie hush as kids thought about what had just happened.

And then a few kids cheered. Others laughed.

Ernie patted me hard on the back. "Guess you passed the test, Matt," he said.

We bumped fists. I was careful to use my left hand. I kept my right hand hidden in the shirtsleeve.

"Back to the party!" someone shouted.

"Back to the party!"

I breathed a long sigh of relief.

Ernie started down the stairs. Then he turned back to me. "Go get your hand," he said. "I'll take you to the Reviver Room."

I nearly choked. "The Reviver Room?"

I remembered how the Reviver Room worked. The high voltage. A shock so powerful it brings the dead back to life.

"A few minutes in the Reviver Room will glue that hand on to stay," Ernie said. "Come on. I'll wait for you."

He turned and clomped down the stairs.

My victory hadn't lasted very long.

I hadn't counted on the Reviver Room. Now, instead of being a smashed egg, I was about to be a *fried* egg.

I made my way slowly down the stairs. I knew I didn't have any more tricks hidden in my pockets.

I tried to come up with a new plan, a new way to fool Ernie. A way to keep him from leading me into that terrifying room.

But my brain froze. I was too frightened to think straight.

I found the rubber hand on the floor against the wall. I quickly tucked it back into the pocket before Ernie could see it clearly.

He motioned to me from an entrance to the court. "Move it, Matt. A few minutes in the Reviver Room. Then you'll be ready to party again."

I . . . don't . . . think . . . so.

I had no choice. I had to follow him.

The music had started up again in the gym. But my heart was pounding faster than the dance music.

From the party, I heard loud voices and kids laughing.

I wasn't laughing.

Ernie led me to the door to the Reviver Room. I struggled to think . . . think of a way to escape. But my brain was letting me down.

Ernie opened the door a crack. I peered inside. Red light filled the room. I saw lots of wires and a wall of electric equipment. I glimpsed a metal chair in front of the equipment.

"I'm kind of hungry," I said. "Maybe we should get something to eat first. Couldn't you go for a few pounds of meat?"

"Fix your hand first," Ernie said, staring at my shirtsleeve. "The longer the hand is off your arm, the longer you'll have to stay in the Reviver Room."

The red light seeped out of the room and washed over me.

Ernie opened the door wide. "The Reviver isn't here," he said. "But we don't need him."

"The Reviver?" I asked. "Maybe we should wait for him to get back."

"He won't be here till morning," Ernie said. "This is an emergency. No worries. Go in."

He motioned me into the room. "Go ahead, Matt," he said. "Take a seat in the Reviver Chair. It's all hooked up. You'll get a good blast."

"A blast?" I uttered. My voice cracked.

"Take your hand and hold it onto the end of your arm," Ernie instructed. "Then . . ."

"Then?" I said. My voice cracked.

"Then I'll throw the switch," Ernie said.

25

I stepped into the red light. It was hot inside the little room. The electric equipment buzzed and crackled.

I gripped the chair back with my one good hand. *"Owww."* The metal felt hot.

"Sit down," Ernie ordered. "What are you waiting for?"

Well . . . I'd just like to take a few more breaths before you FRY me to a crisp.

I started to lower myself onto the hot metal chair. But I stood straight up when I heard voices.

Through the open door, I saw two of Ernie's friends come running up to him.

"Hey — here he is!"

"Ernie — what are you doing here?"

"We've been looking all over for you. Come on, dude. Come back to the party."

"Hurry. The Stomp Contest is starting. We need you, dude."

Ernie tried to explain to them what was happening. But they didn't give him a chance. They pulled him away, back toward the gym.

I stood there holding my breath till I heard the gym doors close behind them. Then I ran out of the Reviver Room.

I slammed the door behind me. I blinked in the bright light.

I couldn't help myself. I lost it. I did a happy dance. "I'm alive! I'm alive! ALIVE!"

I stopped in middance. I suddenly realized the words I was shouting could get me killed.

I glanced up and down the hall. No one there. I could hear the pounding drumbeats of the music in the gym.

I realized my hand was still tucked into my shirtsleeve. I pushed it out and moved the fingers to get the blood flowing.

Tomorrow, I'll tell Ernie I threw the switch myself, I decided. *I'll tell him it worked perfectly, and my hand is back.*

I decided not to return to the party. I wanted to go up to my room and celebrate my good luck.

The kids all thought I was undead now. I had passed the test. I could relax now. No more suspicious stares. No kids following me around, watching my every move.

The rubber hand was a stroke of genius.

"I'm a genius!" I told myself. "A genius!"

"Hey — what are *you* so happy about?" a voice behind me boomed.

I spun around. Angelo.

How long has he been standing there? How much has he heard?

26

I raised my right hand and wiggled the fingers. Then I pointed to the Reviver Room.

"All fixed," I said.

Angelo grabbed my wrist and studied the hand. He turned it over and rubbed his fingers along the skin.

"Wow. Perfect," he said. "You'd never know it fell off."

I nodded. "Yeah. I got lucky," I said.

"Hey, your hand is warm," he said. He eyed me suspiciously.

"From the high voltage," I said.

He nodded. "You going back to the party?"

"No," I said. "All that electricity kind of wiped me out."

"Catch you at practice," Angelo said. He waved good-bye and headed back to the gym.

I couldn't keep a grin from spreading over my face. "Matt, you're definitely a genius!" I told myself.

Guess how long I stayed a genius.

*　　*　　*

The next morning, I woke up with another brilliant idea.

Since the day I arrived at Romero, I noticed something strange and a little creepy about the kids. Most of the undead kids had a pale blue tint to their skin.

I had proved to them at the dance that I was a zombie, too. But I still needed to do everything I could to keep them from guessing the truth about me.

That meant I should have pale blue skin, too.

No problem. I took out my horror-makeup kit. And I very carefully dabbed a blue tint over my face, my neck, and my arms and hands.

When I finished, I checked myself out in the mirror. Yes. The color was perfect. Just a hint of blue.

I got dressed and hurried down the hall. I wanted to show off my skin to Franny. I knew she'd agree that Matt the Genius had struck again.

But she wasn't in her room. She had already gone to breakfast.

I walked through the crowded halls with confidence. No one turned to stare at me. No one followed me, hoping to prove I was alive.

I was accepted. I was one of them.

Everything went perfectly — until gym class.

27

"We're going to run track indoors today," Coach Meadows announced. He blew his whistle. His whole body appeared to deflate every time he blew it.

He had us run laps around the gym. I ran between Angelo and another guy from the soccer team named Steven.

You couldn't really call it running. It was more like stumbling and staggering. Angelo was talking about a soccer match the Vultures were playing against a team called the Spotted Owls.

"Why would anyone name a team that?" Angelo demanded. "What kind of name is Spotted Owls?"

Steven agreed.

"Maybe they don't give a hoot," I joked. I thought it was pretty funny. But neither one of them laughed. I was beginning to catch on that zombies didn't laugh very much.

We ran another lap. Kids trotted slowly, lurching and stumbling. One boy staggered right into the gym wall and then fell flat on his butt. No one seemed to notice.

It felt good to run, even slowly. We didn't get much exercise at this school. I think that's because the undead kids were afraid of body parts falling off.

I let Angelo and Steven run ahead. I wanted a little freedom. A few moments to stretch my muscles and move by myself.

Halfway around the gym again, I thought I saw some kids watching me.

I scolded myself. *Matt, don't start imagining things. You've got them all fooled — remember?*

But I wasn't imagining it. I passed the locker room door and kept trotting. Some boys moved forward to trot right behind me.

I saw others turn and stare.

What was up with that? Just about everyone was staring hard at me now as we all lapped the gym.

My heart started to race. I knew something was wrong. But what could it be?

As I came around again, I grabbed the handle to the locker room door. I pulled the door open and hurried inside.

The air was hot and steamy in the narrow locker room. Someone had left a shower running.

I hurried up to the mirror. I saw kids coming up behind me. What had I done wrong? Why were they chasing after me?

Frantically, I rubbed the mist off the mirror with my hand. I stared into the glass.

I knew instantly that I'd made two mistakes.

The first mistake: I was sweating. Zombies do not sweat.

Mistake number two: The blue makeup. My sweat made the blue makeup run. And it had run onto my white gym T-shirt.

A deep blue stain ran around the collar of the shirt.

I spun around. A large gang of boys had jammed the locker room. Most of them were staring at the sweat pouring down my face and the ring of blue on my shirt.

"Uh . . . this isn't what it looks like," I said. "I mean . . . I was testing something . . . for Halloween. I mean . . ."

My explanation was not going over.

A huge mountain of a kid grabbed the front of my shirt. He rubbed a hand on my sweaty cheeks. And the blue makeup came off on his fingers.

"Uh-oh," he said softly. "Uh-oh. Uh-oh."

28

He pulled my T-shirt tighter. And then he blinked a few times, startled. "Hey — this dude has a heartbeat!" he boomed. "I can hear it. A heartbeat!"

Uh-oh.

No way to talk my way out of this one.

Their angry cries rang out through the steamy air.

I ducked my head and took off. I darted right between the big guy's legs.

Hands grabbed for me. Guys stumbled toward me.

But I ran right through them. That was the one advantage of being alive. I was faster than them.

I rocketed to the locker room door. Shoved it open with both hands and ran full speed into the gym.

A few kids were still trotting around the floor. Coach Meadows looked up. He opened his mouth to call to me. But I was already out of there.

I hurtled out the back door. The afternoon sun was low in the sky. Shielding my eyes, I ran toward the playing fields.

Where was I headed? I didn't know. I only knew I had to get away from these guys.

Glancing back, I saw eight or ten of them come bursting out the back door. They weren't going to give up. They knew they had a living kid in school.

And they didn't want me to stay alive for long.

My sneakers slid on the smooth grass. I ran across the soccer field.

Behind me, they grunted and groaned as they forced their dead legs forward.

I had a good head start. And I could run a lot faster.

But they didn't give up. They just kept coming. Waving their arms in front of them as if ready to grab me at any moment.

I was breathing hard. But my legs felt strong. I knew I could outrun them.

I was nearly across the soccer field when I felt a sharp pain in the back of my head.

I was hit. A soccer ball hit me in the back of the head. I stumbled forward.

Fell hard.

I was down. Down on the grass.

Caught. The zombies had me.

Their ugly grunts and groans grew louder as they staggered toward me.

I raised my head, stunned. Pain rolled down my body. The back of my head throbbed.

"Ohhhh." A low moan escaped my throat as I spread both hands on the grass.

I gave a hard push and forced myself to stand.

Behind me, I glimpsed a zombie kid fall and start to roll toward me. Another guy tripped over him and went down. But several others kept coming, hands outstretched to grab me.

I took a deep breath. I shook off my dizziness and took off again.

But I didn't have far to run.

At the back of the soccer field, I ran right up to the tall black fence. It rose like a wall, high above my head. I glanced from side to side. The fence seemed to stretch forever.

A cry of panic escaped my throat. The groaning zombies moved closer. They had me trapped against the fence.

I turned and started to run full speed. I searched for a door ... a gate ... an opening ... a crack. Anything I could slip through.

Nothing. No way through.

Behind me, I saw a zombie kid stumble and fall. Two kids fell on top of him. The others stopped to help them to their feet.

I spotted a big, square rock poking up from the grass. Catching my balance, I gazed at it for a moment.

Then, I didn't think. I just moved.

I took a few steps back. Came running at the rock. Took a long leap onto it. Hoisted my hands high over my head. And flew up to the top of the fence.

I wrapped both hands over the top — and swung myself up.

"Whooooa!" I uttered a long cry as I sailed over the top of the fence and dropped onto the dirt on the other side.

"Oooof." I landed hard on my back. The collision with the ground knocked the wind from my lungs.

I lay there choking and gasping. I could hear the low groans and muttering from the zombie kids on the other side of the fence.

Did they see me hurtle over the fence?

I was still on my back. I stared up to the top of the fence. I expected to see them follow me over it.

But I heard their clumsy footsteps move along the high fence. Their shouts and groans faded. They hadn't seen me. They kept running.

With a sigh of relief, I stood up. My legs felt shaky. I steadied myself.

I brushed dirt off the front of my clothes and glanced around.

To my surprise, I was standing in a graveyard.

Rows and rows of low gravestones poked up from the flat dirt. The stones were white and looked pretty new.

The graveyard was completely walled in. The fence rose high above me, and I didn't see a door or a gate anywhere.

I was totally boxed in. Yes, I was safe from the zombie kids on the other side. But the sun was going down. Soon, it would be dark.

I didn't want to be trapped in this graveyard in the dark. No way.

I listened hard. The voices on the other side had vanished. Had the zombie kids given up and gone back to the school?

A sudden wind blew through the graveyard, making some of the stones creak. I turned and started to walk between the first two rows of graves.

"Whoa." I stopped about three graves in. Stopped and stared at the name on the tombstone.

Wayne. Angelo's brother.

And the next stone? It was Angelo's.

The twins were buried here. Did that mean all of the zombie Romero kids had their gravestones in this cemetery?

Yes. On the end of the row, I saw Ernie's grave. And a few stones down the stone was engraved for Angelo's friend Mikey.

Each name sent a chill down my back.

The kids were all buried here. But of course most of the graves were empty. Because the kids were undead. Because they had climbed up from their graves and . . . and . . .

I read the name on the next grave and gasped in shock. I froze. My eyes bulged. I had to read the name a second time.

"Oh, noooooo," I moaned. "I . . . don't . . . believe . . . it."

29

Franny's tombstone.

I was staring at Franny's tombstone.

"She lied to me," I murmured.

Franny was a zombie, too. She told me she was alive. She said the two of us were the only living kids at Romero.

Why did she lie?

My mind began to spin. All the things she said to me flashed back into my brain.

She lied. She lied. She lied.

Franny only pretended to be my friend. She only pretended that she wanted to help me.

Why? Because she was watching me the whole time. Spying on me.

That had to be the truth. She pretended to be my friend so she could spy on me for the other zombie kids.

I suddenly felt like a total jerk.

I believed her. I trusted her. I really liked her. She was lying the whole time.

And now here I was, trapped in this grave-yard. Staring at the tombstones of all the kids in the school. Kids who didn't want me to stay alive.

I spun away from Franny's grave. I began walking along the fence. I searched for a way out. And I listened for the zombie kids to return.

But it was silent on the other side. I remembered Franny saying no one ever wanted to come back here because it was so sad and depressing.

She was right.

I made a complete survey of the high fence. No door. No exit of any kind.

I sat down and leaned my back against the fence. I watched the sun slowly drop. Long shadows fell over the graveyard. Then . . . total darkness.

I shivered. The wind was cold and sharp. I hugged my knees and waited.

How long would I be here? Forever?

My stomach growled. I suddenly realized I was starving. In the dark, the tombstones looked like big teeth poking up from the ground.

How late was it? I couldn't tell. The moon was hidden by heavy clouds.

I jumped when I heard a sound nearby. At the fence. A soft *thump*.

Then a scraping sound. Another soft *thump*.

I climbed to my feet and turned toward the sound.

In the gray light, I saw something move on the fence. I couldn't tell what it was. I walked closer. Slowly. Carefully.

It slithered and bumped at the wood planks. I stopped, squinting hard at it.

At first I thought it was a snake. Then I saw *two* of them.

Two long snakes stretching down the wall?

I took a step closer. Then another. No. Not snakes. A rope ladder.

Someone had tossed a rope ladder over the fence. I walked up to it.

"Who's there?" I called.

Silence.

"Who's there?" I repeated. The gusting wind muffled my voice. "Who's there? Who flung this rope ladder down?"

No answer.

I tightened my hands around the sides of the ladder. The rope felt rough against my palms.

I hoisted myself up onto the lowest rung.

"Who's there?" I tried again.

No answer.

Was it a trap?

I had no choice. I couldn't hide in this grave-yard forever. I had to take a chance.

I slid my hands higher and pulled myself to the top.

30

I stared down at Franny, who was holding the other end of the rope ladder.

"Hurry," she whispered. She glanced behind her toward the school. "I guessed where you were hiding. But someone might have followed me."

I scrambled down the ladder. I was happy to be on the other side, out of the graveyard.

I wiped my hands on my shirt. Then I turned to Franny.

The moon floated out from behind the clouds. Moonlight washed over her pale face.

"You lied to me," I said. "You're one of them."

She lowered her eyes. "I know," she replied in a whisper.

"Why?" I asked.

Clouds made her face darken again. She flickered in and out of shadows, like a ghost.

"I had to," she said. "They made me."

She tugged the rope ladder off the wall. She folded it carefully between her hands. Then she tossed it to the ground by the fence.

"It's not safe here," she said. She glanced to the school again.

"Tell me the truth," I insisted. "What do you mean they made you?"

She shrugged her narrow shoulders. "They said I had to spy on you. They need to know about every new kid. Just to make sure a live one doesn't come here by mistake. So . . . it was my turn to spy on the new kid. You."

"I don't understand," I said. "Why did you *help* me? If you were spying on me, why did you help me fool them?"

She glanced away. "I just liked you," she said. "It's been so long since I hung out with a living kid. So I tried to help you keep your secret."

"But —"

She raised a hand to silence me. "They're going to be waiting for you," she said.

I swallowed. "You mean I can't go back to my room?"

"It doesn't matter," she said. "They're going to be waiting for you in the morning. They said they're going to give you the final test. The test to see once and for all if you really are undead."

"Oh, wow." I shook my head. A cold shudder ran down my back.

I grabbed her arm. "Franny — tell me. What's the final test?"

Her eyes locked on mine. "Okay," she whispered. "This is the final test. First, they throw you in the old stone quarry and force you to stay underwater."

"F-for how long?" I stammered.

"At least twenty minutes," she answered. "But there's a lot more, Matt. A kid from the high school is going to run his SUV over you. Then they will throw you off Leapers' Cliff. You know — that rock cliff overlooking town?"

My mouth hung open. I could feel the blood pulsing at my temples.

"That's the final test?" I croaked. "They drown me. They run an SUV over me. And they heave me over a cliff?"

Franny nodded. "A lot of kids pass the test easily."

"But I *can't*!" I cried. "I can't pass that test. I'm *alive*!"

She started walking toward the school. I hurried to catch up to her.

"Franny," I said. "What can I do? How can I survive that test?"

She turned to me, her eyes wide with sadness. "I don't know," she said. "I sure hope you think of something. Good luck, Matt."

31

I sneaked back into my room. I had a few bags of potato chips hidden in a dresser drawer. I gulped them down for my dinner.

I kept all the lights off in case someone came looking for me. I climbed into bed, but I couldn't fall asleep.

My brain was churning. I could almost hear it chugging away in my head, sending out all kinds of crazy thoughts.

There *had* to be a way to survive the test. If only it didn't involve drowning, getting run over, *and* being tossed over a cliff.

I was drenched in sweat. I jumped out of bed in a total panic. It was two in the morning. I knew I'd be awake all night. But I was too frightened to think clearly.

I paced back and forth in my tiny room. Finally, my eyes landed on the rubber hand I'd used at the party. That hand got me out of trouble — at least for a while.

Maybe . . . maybe . . .

I began to get an idea.

What if I distracted them? What if I used my horror makeup and all my horror stuff? What if I did it right this time?

Maybe I could make myself look so much like a zombie, they wouldn't bother with the test.

That was my idea.

A desperate idea, for sure. But what else could I try?

I went to work. I wanted to turn myself into something horrifying, a creature of the undead.

I ripped long gashes in my jeans and T-shirt. I painted a big, blood-soaked open wound on my chest.

I studied it in the mirror. The bleeding wound looked so real, it made my stomach leap.

I dragged out these funny trick shoes my dad bought me in a Hollywood costume store. The shoes were cut in front. They made it look as if my toes had been sliced off.

I sat down in front of the mirror with my makeup kit and fake skin pieces. I worked slowly and carefully. I gave myself the best horror makeup job I'd ever done.

My chin and cheeks dripped with decaying globs of skin. I gave myself one empty eye socket, just a deep black hole where my eye should be. I marked deep gashes in my throat. I put blood-soaked streaks in my hair.

That was all good, but I wasn't finished. I turned one arm into a bloody stump. Then I hid the other arm under my T-shirt.

Nice touch, I thought.

I studied myself in the mirror. "Disgusting," I murmured to myself. "Totally gross and disgusting."

I had turned myself into the most zombie-looking zombie in the history of zombies.

But would it be enough to impress the *real* zombies in my school?

Would it be enough to save my life?

I'd soon find out. It was morning. I opened the door. They were all waiting for me outside my room.

I staggered toward them, my heart pounding.

Could I fool them?

32

I lurched into the hall. I grunted like a zombie. I stared at them with my one good eye.

There had to be at least fifty kids jamming the narrow hall. They had all come to watch me take the big test.

They backed up as I staggered out of my room.

No one spoke. No one made a sound.

Were they shocked? Were they impressed? Was my plan working?

I held my bloodstained stump in front of me and walked like a zombie. Some of the kids were staring at the open wound on my chest. Others studied my decaying, one-eyed face.

Silence.

Why didn't anyone speak?

I realized I had stopped breathing. The suspense was too much for me. I knew my life was on the line.

I let my breath out in a long *whoosh*.

Still silence.

And then . . . a boy started to laugh.

The laughter spread quickly. In seconds, everyone was laughing.

I gasped. Waves of laughter rang out. Loud, high-pitched laughter that echoed down the long, narrow hall.

"Hey — what's so funny?" I choked out.

But they were laughing too loud to hear me. And suddenly, I was being lifted off the floor.

Angelo and his friend Mikey hoisted me onto their shoulders. My head nearly bumped the ceiling.

Kids cheered and laughed some more. They clapped and bumped fists. Angelo and Mikey carried me down the hall. Everyone followed. Like a big parade.

But — why? Why were they laughing? I was desperate to know.

Did it mean I was okay? Did it mean they weren't going to drown me, run over me, and toss me off a cliff?

What was so funny?

If only they would *tell* me!

And then I heard something that made me *choke*. I heard a girl shout: "Take him to the Reviver Room!"

That made kids start to laugh again. Angelo and Mikey gripped my legs and bounced me on their shoulders. We turned the corner and headed down the stairs.

"The Reviver Room!"

"Fix him! Revive him!"

"Reviver Room! Reviver Room!"

Their cheers and cries followed us down the stairs. Now we were leading the way down the hall past the gym.

"Wait! Stop!" I screamed. I couldn't hide my panic. My voice burst out high and shrill.

I looked down at Angelo. "Why?" I cried. "Why are you taking me there?"

"You're totally messed up, Matt," Angelo said. "You're wounded and you're decaying."

"You're coming apart," Mikey chimed in. "The Reviver Room will restore you. It will put you back together."

No, it won't! I thought. *The Reviver Room won't restore me. It'll KILL me!*

My makeup job was TOO GOOD.

"Put me down!" I cried. "Come on, guys! Put me down!"

The two big hulks gripped my legs tightly. They ignored my pleas.

The door to the Reviver Room came into view.

If only they'd put me down, I could make a run for it. Maybe hide in a closet or something till my parents came to get me.

"Put me down! Let me walk there!" I screamed. I twisted and squirmed. I tried to kick my way free.

But Angelo and Mikey held tight and refused to let me down.

We stopped in front of the Reviver Room door. A girl pulled it open. And the two boys heaved me into the room.

I stumbled toward the metal chair in the middle of the room. The red light washed over me as I struggled to catch my balance.

In the hall, the kids cheered and laughed. Then the door slammed shut, and I was left in silence.

My heart thudded in my chest. I turned to the door. I pounded on it with both fists.

"Let me out! Let me OUT of here!" I screamed. "I quit! I QUIT zombie school! Let me out! I QUIT!"

Could they hear me out in the hall? I don't think so.

I grabbed the door handle. I pushed it. Then I pulled it. The door didn't budge.

I gasped when I heard a cough.

I spun around and glared into the red light. I wasn't alone in there.

An old man with a scratched-up bald head and a scraggly white beard stood watching me from the back wall. I squinted hard. Part of his nose was missing, and he had only one ear.

He studied me silently. Then he raised a pair of handcuffs.

"Who — who are you?" I stammered.

"I'm the Reviver," he replied in a scratchy old-man's voice. "Sit down. Come."

He motioned to the metal chair with the handcuffs. "Sit down. Only take a few seconds," he said. "Make you all better."

33

"Uh . . . I don't belong in here," I choked out. I was shaking so hard, I could barely speak.

The old man stared at my face. I guess he was looking at the deep ruts, the decayed lumps of skin, the missing eye.

"I'm not a zombie," I said.

"Fix you up," he repeated. He waved the handcuffs. "Sit. Only hurts a little while. Then, make you all better."

He stepped closer. "What's a little pain, kid? You already dead — right?"

He didn't give me a chance to answer. He grabbed my shoulders and pushed me down on the chair. He looked old and feeble. But he had amazing strength.

I glanced around the tiny closet of a room. Nowhere to run. No way to escape.

"Make you all better," the Reviver muttered again. "Only hurts little while."

I froze in panic. I couldn't move. I shut my eyes. I really didn't want to see what happened next.

Next thing I knew, I was handcuffed to the chair with a metal helmet on my head.

I twisted around and saw the Reviver step up to a big black switch on the back wall. "I be more careful this time," he said.

"Huh? Careful?"

He nodded. "Too much power. Last boy end up as burned toast. I be more careful."

He didn't give me a chance to reply.

He raised his hand and pulled down the switch.

34

I shut my eyes. I gritted my teeth so hard, my whole jaw hurt.

I heard a loud hum.

Then I gasped as a buzz shot through my body. Whoa. Wait. It was weak. It didn't hurt at all. Just a mild tingle. It died after a few seconds.

I opened my eyes. I started to breathe again.

"No juice!" the Reviver screamed angrily. He slammed the wall with his fist. "No juice! No juice! The machine — *busted*!"

He stepped up to my chair and raised the helmet from my head. Then he clicked open the handcuffs.

"No juice," he repeated, shaking his bald head. "I use it up on burned toast kid."

I started to jump up. But he pushed me back into the chair.

"Sit still," he said. "I fix machine. I fix. A few minutes. Then we will try again."

I hunched in the chair. I felt weak from fright. I had survived — so far.

But now what?

Every once in a while, a kid has to be *brilliant* — right?

Every once in a while, a kid has to have a brilliant idea.

Now it was *my* turn to be brilliant. I had an idea.

I jumped up from the chair. "It *worked*!" I cried happily.

I did a little dance. I leaped up and down. I pranced around the chair. "It worked!" I shouted. "I'm revived! Look! I'm all fixed! I'm revived!"

I wiped the black makeup off my eye. I poked my hand out from my shirtsleeve.

The old man looked up from the controls on the back wall. He squinted at me. "It worked?"

"Yes!" I cried happily. "Yes!" I jumped up and down some more. I pumped my fists in the air. "Thank you! You saved me!"

The Reviver stepped up to me. He pinched my arm. Then he pinched my nose.

"Yes. You are fixed," he said. "I see you are like new."

"Thank you," I said again.

"Go, go, go," he said. "Go back to class. See you again."

I don't think so, I thought.

A week later, I started my new school.

How did I convince my parents to let me out of zombie school?

It wasn't easy. But come on. I was clever enough to fool the zombies. So I was also smart enough to convince my parents I needed out.

Actually, I just begged and begged till they said okay.

Now here I was walking down the shiny, bright halls of my brand-new boarding school. Safe and sound. No undead kids following me around. No zombies anywhere in sight.

Wow.

A fresh start. New kids. New teachers. A whole new life.

Was I happy? Was I excited? Do you even have to ask?

I stepped up to a shiny silver water fountain and bent my head to take a drink.

Whoa. Wait. I jerked my head back as a thick red liquid poured from the faucet.

Was the fountain rusty?

I stepped away from the fountain and continued walking. The Dining Hall was at the end of the corridor.

I peeked inside. Kids sat at tables drinking from big bowls. I stepped closer. The bowls all contained a red liquid.

Weird.

I turned back to the door. A man in a brown suit strode up to me. "I'm the dean of students. Are you Matt Krinsky?" he asked. When he spoke, small, pointed fangs pointed down from his upper lip.

"Uh . . . yes," I said.

He stuck out his hand. "Welcome to Dracula Middle School," he said.

WELCOME BACK TO
THE HALL OF HORRORS

Well, Matt. Fangs for telling me your story. Bad news. Sounds like your new school may be a *pain in the neck*!

Sorry. I like to have my little joke. Your zombie school may not have put you on the Honor Roll. But it certainly put you on the Horror Roll.

Thank you for bringing your story to me. I am the Story-Keeper, and I will keep your story here in the Hall of Horrors where it belongs.

And now, here comes a new guest. What is your name? Jack Harmon?

Why did you bring that cell phone, Jack?

"There's someone inside it. Someone in the phone telling me to do horrible, dangerous things."

Maybe it's just a wrong number, Jack. But sit down. You've come to the right place. In the Hall of Horrors, There's Always Room for One More Scream.

Ready for More?

Here's another tale from the Hall of Horrors:

DON'T SCREAM!

1

"YOWWWWWWWWW!"

That's me, Jack Harmon, screaming my head off. I was on the school bus, heading home, howling in pain. As usual.

You would scream too if Mick Owens had you in an armlock. Mick shoved my arm up behind me till I heard my bones and muscles snap and pop.

"YOWWWWWWW!" I repeated.

Nothing new here. Big Mick and his friend Darryl "The Hammer" Oliva like to beat me up, tease me, and torture me on the bus every afternoon.

Last week, our sixth grade teacher, Miss Harris, had a long, serious talk in class about bullying. I guess Mick and Darryl were out that day.

Otherwise, they would know that bullying is bad.

Why do they do it? Because I'm smaller than them? Because I'm a skinny little guy who looks like a third-grader? Because I scream easily?

No.

These two super-hulks like to get up in my face because it's FUN.

They think it's funny. It makes them laugh. You should see the big grins on their faces whenever I beg and plead for them to pick on someone their own size.

And then, as soon as I start to scream, it's belly-laugh time for those two losers.

One day, I complained to Charlene, the school bus driver. But she said, "I'm a bus driver—not a referee."

Not too helpful.

And so here we were in the narrow aisle at the back of the bus. Mick with a big grin on his red, round-cheeked face. Me with my arm twisted behind my back.

Darryl watched from his seat. The other kids on the bus faced forward, pretending nothing was happening.

"YOWWWWWWW!"

Mick swiped his big fist at my head—and tugged off my Red Sox cap.

"Hey—give it back!" I cried. I made a grab for it. But he sent it sailing across the aisle to Darryl.

Darryl caught it and waved it at me. "Nice cap, dude."

I dove for it. Stumbled and fell halfway down the aisle. Darryl passed my cap back to his good buddy.

I turned, breathing hard. "Give it back."

"It's MY cap now," Mick said. He slapped it onto his curly blond hair. His head is so big, the cap didn't fit.

I dove again, hands outstretched. I almost grabbed the cap back, but Mick heaved it to Darryl. I swung around to Darryl, and he tossed it over my head back to Mick.

The bus slowed, then bumped to a stop. I bounced hard into the back of my seat. I glanced out the window. We were at Mick's house.

"Give me my Red Sox cap," I said. I stuck out my hand.

"You want it?" Mick grinned at me. "You really want it? Here."

He held the cap upside down in front of him and spit into it. A big white sticky glob.

"Here," he said. "You still want it?"

I stared into the cap. Stared at the disgusting white glob of spit.

Darryl hee-hawed like a donkey. He thinks everything Mick does is a riot.

"You still want your cap?" Mick repeated. He held it out of my reach. "Tell you what, Jacko. Give me your watch and you can have your cap."

"That's totally fair," Darryl said.

"No way!" I cried. "My grandfather gave me this watch. No way!"

The watch was a special present for my twelfth birthday. It means a lot to me. I never take it off.

"How about it, Jacko?" Mick stuck his hand out. "The watch for your Red Sox cap."

"Yo, Mick. See your house outside the window?" Charlene yelled from behind the wheel. "You want to keep us all here till dinnertime? What's your mom serving us?"

A few kids laughed at that. But most kids are too terrified of Mick to ever laugh around him.

"Mick, stop torturing Jack," Charlene yelled. "Give him back his cap and get off my bus!"

"Okay, okay. No problem," Mick said with a sneer.

He jammed the cap onto my head, so hard my feet nearly went through the bus floor. I could feel the sticky glob of spit in my hair.

Mick trotted to the door at the front. Darryl gave me a friendly punch in the ribs. Then he followed his buddy off the bus.

I let out a long sigh of relief. I had survived another trip home on the school bus. I watched Mick and Darryl jog up the driveway to Mick's little redbrick house. They punched each other as they ran. You know. Kidding around.

I slumped into the nearest seat. I shut my eyes and took a deep breath.

No permanent wounds. That meant it was a good day.

Glancing down, I saw something on the seat next to me. A silvery cell phone.

I hesitated for a moment, just staring at it. Then I reached over and picked up the phone.

And that's when the nightmare began.

About the Author

R.L. Stine's books are read all over the world. So far, his books have sold more than 300 million copies, making him one of the most popular children's authors in history. Besides Goosebumps, R.L. Stine has written the teen series Fear Street and the funny series Rotten School, as well as the Mostly Ghostly series, The Nightmare Room series, and the two-book thriller *Dangerous Girls*. R.L. Stine lives in New York with his wife, Jane, and Minnie, his King Charles spaniel. You can learn more about him at www.RLStine.com.

NEED MORE THRILLS?

Get Goosebumps!

PLAY

Wii

PlayStation 2

Nintendo DS

WATCH

Goosebumps: NIGHT IN TERROR TOWER

Goosebumps: ONE DAY AT HORRORLAND

Goosebumps: MONSTER BLOOD

LISTEN

SCHOLASTIC

www.scholastic.com/goosebumps

The Original Bone-Chilling Series

—with Exclusive Author Interviews!

NIGHT of the LIVING DUMMY

R.L. STINE

SCHOLASTIC

DEEP TROUBLE

R.L. STINE

SCHOLASTIC

MONSTER BLOOD

R.L. STINE

SCHOLASTIC

the HAUNTED MASK

R.L. STINE

SCHOLASTIC

ONE DAY at HORRORLAND

R.L. STINE

SCHOLASTIC

the CURSE of the MUMMY'S TOMB

R.L. STINE

SCHOLASTIC

BE CAREFUL WHAT YOU WISH FOR

R.L. STINE

SCHOLASTIC

SAY CHEESE and DIE!

R.L. STINE

SCHOLASTIC

the HORROR at CAMP JELLYJAM

R.L. STINE

SCHOLASTIC

HOW I GOT MY SHRUNKEN HEAD

R.L. STINE

SCHOLASTIC

■ SCHOLASTIC

www.scholastic.com/goosebumps

GBCL2

R. L. Stine's Fright Fest!
Now with Splat Stats and More!

REVENGE OF THE LIVING DUMMY
R.L. STINE
SCHOLASTIC

CREEP FROM THE DEEP
R.L. STINE
SCHOLASTIC

MONSTER BLOOD FOR BREAKFAST!
R.L. STINE
SCHOLASTIC

THE SCREAM OF THE HAUNTED MASK
R.L. STINE
SCHOLASTIC

DR. MANIAC VS. ROBBY SCHWARTZ
R.L. STINE
SCHOLASTIC

WHO'S YOUR MUMMY?
R.L. STINE
SCHOLASTIC

MY FRIENDS CALL ME MONSTER
R.L. STINE
SCHOLASTIC

SAY CHEESE - AND DIE SCREAMING!
R.L. STINE
SCHOLASTIC

WELCOME TO CAMP SLITHER
R.L. STINE
SCHOLASTIC

SCHOLASTIC

www.EnterHorrorLand.com

GBHL19I

GOOSEBUMPS®
HALL OF HORRORS

THERE'S ALWAYS ROOM FOR ONE MORE SCREAM!

An all-new series from fright-master R.L. Stine!